THE ARDAGH EMERALDS

England in the 1890s. The world of Victoria and the Empire. This is the world, too, of AJ Raffles, man about town, who, assisted by his inept assistant Bunny Manders, is a successful jewel thief. The eight stories in this book recapture the spirit of the Naughty Nineties, when the gentleman burglar would put out his Sullivan cigarette, don a black mask, outwit a villain, and save a lady in distress — and all before going out to dinner!

JOHN HALL

THE ARDAGH EMERALDS

Complete and Unabridged

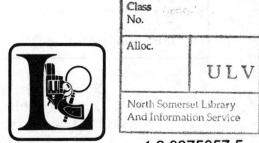
LINFORD
Leicester

First published in Great Britain

First Linford Edition
published 2007

This novel is a work of fiction. Characters and names are the product of the author's imagination. Any resemblance to anybody, living or dead, is entirely coincidental

British Library CIP Data

Hall, John, *1948 –*
    The Ardagh emeralds.—Large print ed.—
Linford mystery library
    1. Raffles (Fictitious character)—Fiction
    2. Jewel thieves—Fiction
    3. Detective and mystery stories
    4. Large type books
    I. Title
    823.9'14 [F]

ISBN 978–1–84617–867–2

Published by
F. A. Thorpe (Publishing)
Anstey, Leicestershire

Set by Words & Graphics Ltd.
Anstey, Leicestershire
Printed and bound in Great Britain by
T. J. International Ltd., Padstow, Cornwall

This book is printed on acid-free paper

For Lesley

1

THE ARDAGH EMERALDS

Rogue though I am, I have my scruples, my own standards. I have resolved that if I am to write further tales of my friend the late AJ Raffles, they will be tales of him as he was at his best, before disgrace had come to us both, before I had served my eighteen months in Wormwood Scrubs, and Raffles, broken in health though he never would and never could be broken in spirit, was hiding under a false name.

And, too, they will be plain unvarnished tales. Like some of my more illustrious literary colleagues, I have on occasion been compelled to be somewhat equivocal as to all the details of Raffles' exploits. The need for such deviousness is gone now — would that it were not! — gone with Raffles himself, and as a consequence I can tell the whole truth here.

One of the instances where I was less than honest was the little matter of the Ardagh emeralds, which I dismissed in passing with the statement that it was a 'dull affair.' That was not entirely true, as you shall see; and you shall see too that there was good reason for my lack of veracity.

It was some six or seven weeks after the stirring events at Milchester, which I have recorded elsewhere in my tales of Raffles. The autumnal equinox was a month in the past, and the evenings were shortening, and starting to produce that slight chill which makes a man think of his own mortality, and of the need to look in his wardrobe for a warmer jacket.

I had gone round to Raffles' rooms in the Albany one evening, and found that he was out. I was in that sort of reflective, even sombre, mood to which I have just referred, and I lit a cigar, poured a brandy and soda, and sat at the window, staring out at the street lights and musing on what Mr Pickwick called the strange mutability of human existence — at least, I think it was Mr Pickwick, though the

2

exact reference escapes me. In short, I was half dozing and half wondering what the winter might bring. Truth to tell, I dared not think too much about the next few months, for my share of the proceeds of the Milchester robbery had been spent, and my finances were in a more than usually parlous state. And I knew that Raffles was in much the same boat, so it looked as if we should be obliged to resume that life of crime which had been in abeyance since August.

It was with something of a start that I came fully to my senses. The door had just opened and closed, interrupting my reveries, and before I could properly struggle to my feet Raffles was in the room, and hailing me cheerfully. 'Another brandy, Bunny? A Sullivan, perhaps?'

I waved the stump of my cigar at him. 'Perhaps another brandy, though, as long as you've got the decanter unstoppered.'

He handed me a drink, and sat down facing me. 'Know much about Ireland, Bunny?' he asked casually.

'Ireland?' I frowned, trying to recollect what, if anything, I did know about it.

'Lots of rain, I understand, and a very green sort of place as a result. 'The Emerald Isle', don't they call it?'

Raffles gave a little start, which another observer might easily have missed.

'Raffles?'

'Rather curious that you should recall that old phrase, that's all, Bunny.'

'How's that, Raffles?'

'I met old Lord Ardagh at the club this evening,' he said. 'His wife has some very fine emeralds, you know.'

'Yes, they are quite famous.' I stared at him. 'I trust — '

Raffles interrupted me. 'We are invited to Ardagh Castle for a week or two,' he said, in the most casual way imaginable. He smiled at me, and added, 'Can you get away in the next day or so?' And he lit a cigarette, and blew a perfect smoke ring towards the ceiling.

My mind was in a whirl. 'Ardagh Castle? Us, go to Ireland? But why? And I trust you are not thinking about those emeralds, Raffles?'

'Ah, when you ask, 'why', Bunny, I fear you have me. Old Ardagh said by way of preamble that he had seen me playing at Lord's this summer, but when I pointed out that the cricket season is over, he became somewhat vague. 'Just a small gathering, fairly informal', was how he put it.' And he blew another smoke ring.

I nodded, half understanding, for it was by no means uncommon for Raffles to be asked to make up numbers at parties, or dinner tables, or what have you. Handsome, urbane, an excellent speaker with a fund of anecdotes, he was an asset to any social gathering. I could not quite make out, though, why I had been invited along. 'Are you sure I'm invited? And are you thinking about those emeralds?' I asked him.

'Oh, you're invited all right, Bunny. 'Bring along that young chap who's always with you', that's what our host told me.'

I persisted. 'And the emeralds?'

'Ah.' Raffles blew one last smoke ring, and pitched the stub of his Sullivan into the fire. 'I will confess that the emeralds played their small part in settling the question of whether I should accept the invitation for both of us. I cannot well say whether the opportunity will arise to avail ourselves of the sparklers, but one can hope. One must hope, for unless something turns up soon, things will be unconscionably difficult.'

'They will indeed! 'The winter of our discontent', is the phrase that comes to mind.'

Raffles stared at me. 'You are in a reflective, if not a dismal, mood. Perhaps the fresh air of the Irish countryside will dispel it, though. Well, are you busy, or will you accompany me?'

'Oh, I'll go with you, no doubt of that. When do we leave?'

'The end of the week. Ardagh is leaving tomorrow, and he promised to have everything ready for our arrival.'

I hardly needed two or three days to pack my few possessions, and Friday morning saw us on the train for Liverpool. A short sea crossing, a slow little local train that stopped for no reason at all every few miles in the midst of bogs and heather, and late on Saturday afternoon we were in a donkey cart being

6

could not have done better at the most expensive restaurants in London or Paris. And the conversation, too, was exceptional, for Lord Ardagh had a remarkable fund of stories, all of them quite suitable for mixed company. He had evidently travelled extensively in his youth, and his anecdotes of people and places were amusing and instructive without being in the slightest degree indelicate. I was seated between Lady Alice and Freddie, and opposite Raffles and Lady Patricia. I must say that I enjoyed myself greatly, but Raffles seemed to be having an uphill task keeping Lady Patricia amused. My friend was on the very top of his form, and yet Lady Patricia turned but a very dull eye upon him; so much so that were it not for Lord Ardagh's conversation, things would have been very quiet. As I say, our host kept things going, and I suspect that nobody but myself had noticed the slight strain that appeared to exist between Raffles and Lady Patricia.

Later in the evening, when the ladies had gone upstairs, Lord Ardagh, his son, Raffles and I went into the billiard room, and we played a few games. Lord Ardagh was the first to excuse himself, and as the door closed after him, Raffles turned to me and said, 'You're looking a bit tired, too, Bunny.'

'Am I? That's odd. Never felt more wide awake, Raffles!'

'Yes, you look decidedly peaky. The long journey, I expect. Best get off to bed, old chap, for you recall that we are pledged to take Lady Patricia riding first thing tomorrow.'

This was the first I had heard of any such engagement, but Raffles' tone and the slight lift of one eyebrow were all the prompting I needed. 'Now you mention it, I am a touch fatigued, Raffles. Yes, I think I'll turn in.' And off I went upstairs.

Of course I did not turn in, but instead lit a cigar and sat in an armchair, until such time as Raffles should come and tell me what he had discovered from the unsuspecting Freddie.

It did not take long, some fifteen or twenty minutes at the outside, and then Raffles threw open my door and strode in with a look of thunder on his usually serene features.

'What is it, old fellow?' I asked solicitously.

He threw himself into a chair and lit a Sullivan. 'I'll tell you what it is, Bunny,' he said. 'Why do you think I was invited here, then?'

I shook my head. 'Can't imagine.'

'I was asked here to play the part of — of a gigolo, Bunny! Nothing more nor less than that!'

'Oh. We had a jolly good dinner, though,' was all that I could manage to stammer out.

Poor though it was, it brought the shadow of a smile to Raffles' face. 'Dash it all Bunny,' said he, 'you put the price of my honour deuced low!'

Before I could think of any response to this, there was an apologetic sort of tap at the door. 'Come in!' I said, and the door opened a fraction and the head of Viscount Mourne appeared in the opening.

Freddie looked as if he had been thoroughly enjoying himself, until he had a sudden shock and sobered up pretty quickly. I'm sure you will have seen the look on your own face in the mirror often enough to know just what I mean. If I had stammered earlier, Freddie positively bleated. 'I say!' he began. And when he had insinuated himself a few inches further through the door, 'I never — that is to say — I mean — the old man — ' and he flushed and shuffled his feet.

Raffles never spoke. He merely crooked a finger to indicate a chair, and Freddie sank into it with a palpable sigh of relief. 'Look here,' said Freddie when he was settled at his ease, or as close thereto as he could manage, 'I thought I'd follow you here, try to explain. You shot off without letting me tell you the full story, and — '

'You forget,' I said, 'that so far I haven't even had half the story, unlike Raffles here, so perhaps you'd better start at the very beginning, for my benefit?'

'Yes, of course, absolutely.' Freddie accepted the cigarette which Raffles offered him, and set off again. 'Right. My sister — Patricia, you know? — has formed an attachment, a romantic attachment, to — or is that 'with'? — anyway,

14

she's fallen for one of the local chaps hereabouts, one Charlie Moran. Son of the tobacco bloke, you know.'

'What, 'Moran's Mountain Mixture'?' I asked.

'The same.' You'll have smoked this popular blend, I know; the tin has a green label showing misty mountains far away, chaps cutting turf in the middle distance, and in the foreground a poor but honest peasant puffing contentedly at an old clay pipe. A legend to the general effect, 'Made in Belfast: Generously flavoured with Latakia and mellow with age,' completes the picture; whether this means the tobacco or the peasant is not for me to say.

'He's rolling in it, of course,' Freddie added. 'Comes in for the whole shooting match in due course.' And he stared into space more morosely than this statement would appear to warrant.

'I feel that your account is accurate thus far, but perhaps the slightest touch incomplete,' prompted Raffles gently.

'Ah. Right. Well, old Charlie's a good fellow, and all that, but he's Irish, you see.'

'Yes?'

Freddie sighed. 'You see, it's this way. The old man — I mean, all these Anglo-Irish chaps, especially the aristocracy, have some tendency to eccentricity, but the old man's way ahead of the field in the oddity stakes. More English than the English, as it were. And a dashed sight more conservative than — I don't know, than the Prime Minister,' he added, waving a hand to emphasize the point.

'You still leave me wondering,' said Raffles.

'Well, he's got a bee in his bonnet about Pat marrying an Englishman, that's all.'

'Ah!'

'And it doesn't help one bit that Charlie has an equally large bee about the cause of Irish independence.'

'I begin to see.'

'Not that he's a Fenian, or anything,' added Freddie rather hastily. 'But one can sympathize with the objects, and still disapprove of the means.'

'Just so. Let me see if I read the situation correctly,' said Raffles. 'You said

that your sister had formed an attachment, which suggests that Mr Charles
Moran is not entirely unwilling?'

'Oh, he's keen as mustard.'

'But your father is averse to the match?'

'Yes.'

'Now, since Mr Moran junior is, in
your expressive phrase, 'coming in for the
whole shooting match' in due course, I
must confess that the fundamental
difficulty escapes me. Granted, there may
well be some initial strain in the relations
between your father and your sister — '

Freddie silenced him with a wave of the
hand. 'No, you miss the point, old chap.
Or at any rate, you haven't the full picture
yet. For one thing, Pat wouldn't want any
strained relations, as you call them, with
the old man, for she worships him
— apart from this one little quirk, that is.
And there's another thing, which is far
more to the point. You see, the fact of
Charlie's inheriting the business and the
cash and what have you is, what can I call
it, conditional upon his keeping his nose
clean. Should he fail in that regard, his
father — another eccentric — would cut

him off without the proverbial shilling.'

'Mr Moran senior also disapproves of the match, then?'

'I don't believe he even knows about it,' said Freddie. 'And I think he'd be delighted if he did.'

Raffles frowned. 'Again, you lose me, young Freddie.'

'Well, the old man has this thing about Pat marrying an Englishman, but that's all, he doesn't dislike the Irish in any way. In point of fact, he and Charlie's father are the best of friends, and also business partners, for the old man has shares in the tobacco works.'

'Ah!'

'So you see that the old man is in a position to exert considerable influence, both personal and financial, upon Mr Moran senior. Influence which he will not hesitate to exert, I may add. See it all now?'

'The picture does begin to grow a little clearer.'

'And if Charlie is disowned, and Pat's disowned — well! I mean to say, old Charlie's a good fellow and all that, but

18

he's no more adapted to working for a living than you or I.'

'I say!' I began hotly, but Raffles silenced me with a look.

'The crux, then, is Lord Ardagh? If he might be persuaded to approve of the match, there would be no further difficulty?'

'You sum it up admirably,' agreed Freddie. 'Trouble is, the old man would never be persuaded.'

I had followed all this complicated to and fro business pretty well thus far, and now had, I trust, a reasonable grasp of the situation as it stood. But something was nagging at me; I felt that some vital information had thus far failed to surface, and it was at this point, as a gloomy sort of silence fell upon the three of us, that I remembered what it was. 'I say!' I said. 'This is all very well, young Freddie, but where exactly does Raffles come into all this? That's what you started to tell me, and you haven't told me yet!'

'Ah, yes, Raffles,' said Freddie, with a ghastly grin of embarrassment. 'I almost forgot. You see, old Moran has works not only in Belfast but in Liverpool as well. Import and export and distribution, and all that,' he added vaguely. 'Anyway, the idea is that Charlie should go over there, learn that end of the business. He leaves in a couple of weeks, and will be there until next spring. The old man's idea, if I have read it aright — for he hasn't exactly confided in me, you understand — is that Raffles here will distract Pat for the next couple of weeks, until Charlie has taken his leave.'

'In the hope that absence will make her heart grow fonder — of somebody else?' said Raffles.

'Just so. There'll be Christmas parties coming up, and hunt balls, and things, and the old man will introduce Pat to as many eligible Englishmen as he can, in the hope that one will click before Charlie returns. If not, then he'll whisk her off to London for the season, and give Charlie the miss in baulk.'

I was almost overcome with sheer delight, but with a struggle I kept my voice as level as I could in the circumstances. 'And you did say that

Raffles would only be needed for a couple of weeks, until Charlie takes his leave?' I asked innocently. 'A sort of temporary shift or contrivance? A fleeting distraction, in fact?'

Raffles shot me a venomous look, but Freddie merely looked more embarrassed than ever. 'It's an awful cheek, I know,' he said. 'My fault, I should never have mentioned it in the first place. I don't know what the old man will say when he finds out that I did.'

Raffles' mood changed at once. 'No need for him to find out at all,' he said cheerily. 'Bunny and I won't say anything, of course, and I expect you'd rather not mention it to your father?'

Freddie stared at him. 'You mean — I thought you'd be leaving, once you knew? Are you — that is, are you staying, after all?'

Raffles nodded. 'And this conversation will be just between the three of us, if you don't mind?'

'Oh, absolutely! Absolutely! I mean — well, thanks awfully,' And Freddie, burbling the same sentiment over and over, allowed himself to be gently but firmly ushered out into the corridor.

When the door had at last closed upon the unfortunate Freddie, Raffles turned to me, a glint in his eye. 'Well?'

'Well, are we staying? In your position, I think I'd have sent for the butler at once and told him to pack my bags.'

Raffles managed a laugh. 'That was, I confess, my first thought. But on reflection we may be as well staying.'

'Freddie was right, though, it is a frightful cheek.'

'It is,' agreed Raffles. He lit a Sullivan and blew out a smoke ring. Then he smiled at me. 'To be fair, I must say that the scheme as outlined by Freddie, in itself and of itself, as it were, is not without a specious kind of merit. In fact, had old Ardagh had the rudimentary decency to approach me directly and give his side of the story, I might well have been tempted to go along with it. But to find out like this at second hand, not to be trusted sufficiently to be let into the game, is a different matter altogether. 'Temporary contrivance', indeed!'

'Those were my words, Raffles,' I reminded him.

'True, but they are pretty clearly Lord Ardagh's sentiments. No, Bunny, our host has, I fear, lost any sympathy I may have had for him under different circumstances. I shall have no compunction now about taking the emeralds.'

'The emeralds?' I gasped.

'You hadn't forgotten them, I trust?'

'Now you mention it, they had rather slipped my mind in all the excitement. But more to the point, Raffles, is that it has obviously slipped your mind that we are the only guests here!' This was, as you have doubtless gathered from my description of events so far, literally true. The castle was well lit, well heated, bright and light and all the rest — but only where we happened to be. Nine tenths of the place was dark and shut up. A far cry, this, from the usual country house party where there are a score or more guests, who may be relied upon to dilute, so to speak, any suspicion that may be going!

Raffles gazed at me in silence for a long moment, drumming his fingers upon the mantel shelf. 'You acknowledge a major obstacle there, Bunny,' he said at last. 'Very well, then, I shall content myself with stealing his daughter!'

'Raffles!'

'Oh, purely metaphorically speaking, old chap. As an agent, as it were, for the worthy Mr Charles Moran.' And he nodded a good night, and left me standing there open-mouthed.

The various revelations of the evening should, perhaps, have unsettled my mind to the extent that I was unable to sleep. I have to say, though, that such was not the case. Whether it was the journey, which had been long and tiring, just as Raffles had said earlier; or whether those very revelations had overtaxed my poor brain, I know not. I can only say that I was off to sleep as soon as I got into bed, and knew no more until eight next morning.

Breakfast, I was pleased to discover, was an informal affair. So informal, indeed, that I was alone at the table. The butler looked in for a while, and as I finished my meal Freddie appeared, looking very much the worse for wear;

but of our host and hostess, Lady Patricia, or Raffles, there was no sign.

Freddie nodded a greeting and winced, evidently at the effect produced by the movement of his head. 'I thought Raffles promised to take Pat out riding?' he complained.

'Did he?'

'So Pat just said, as she stormed past me in the devil of a temper. Said he'd gone out at some ungodly hour, though I don't know how she knows. From the servants, I expect.' He regarded the impressive array of dishes on the sideboard and shuddered. 'Just coffee, I think.'

Frankly I was in no mood to listen to the young ass, and anyway he looked as if he would be best left alone for an hour or two, so I grunted something or the other and set off outside and down the drive, seeing nobody as I went.

At the huge iron gates, I halted irresolute. I did not know the district in the slightest, and I had not the least idea as to which direction Raffles might have taken. Had Lady Patricia not been in such a hurry, or not been so keen on the notion of Raffles and none other taking her riding, I might have offered my services there, but that possibility had gone.

A passing farm labourer regarded me with open curiosity, and ventured the opinion that it was a fine day. I agreed that such was the case, and asked which way the village was. He pointed the road out to me, and I set off, in no hurry to do anything in particular.

The tiny village, 'hamlet,' I think is more the word, of Ardagh lies about half a mile from the castle itself. I called in at the little tobacconist's shop and bought a tin of Moran's Mountain Mixture — from what one might call sentimental motives — then sat on a primitive bench of sorts outside the diminutive church and smoked for a time. There was little traffic on the road, but I was told that it was a fine day by, in turn, the vicar — who scrounged a fill of my tobacco — two aged rustics, and an attractive girl with the characteristic red hair of the country, and a look in her eye which spoke of a marked liveliness of disposition. It was as I was staring down the lane after this last passer-by that I felt a hand on my shoulder, and glanced round to see Raffles standing there.

'A fine day, Bunny.'

'So they all tell me. Where have you been, Raffles?'

'Oh,' said he vaguely, 'I thought it might be as well to have a word with this Charlie Moran.'

'And did you?'

'I did. A nice young chap, Bunny, and good-looking in a rough-hewn way, though not remarkable for any great intelligence. Make someone an ideal husband.'

'And what did he have to say for himself, then?'

'This and that,' he replied with that same irritating vagueness. 'He did point me in the direction of what in London I suppose would be called a night-club, though here they call it a shebeen.'

'What, an illegal drinking den? I trust you didn't try the local poteen, though! Lethal, they say.'

'Something of an acquired taste, I allow. But it was not that I sought, Bunny.'

'Oh?' I frowned. 'Anyway, I'm surprised they let you in, being English and all.'

'I rather pride myself on my Irish accent, you know.'

'Oh, really! I trust it's a jolly sight better than your Cockney!'

He regarded me severely. 'Bunny, Bunny! In any event it was good enough to fool a couple of very rough-looking characters who stood next to me and aired their grievances.' He approached a little closer, and lowered his voice. 'The fact is, Bunny, I overheard these chaps talking about blowing up the barracks!'

I fairly gasped at this. 'Good Lord! Fenians, I suppose. We must alert the authorities — but perhaps you have already done that?'

He shook his head. 'I planned to tell Lord Ardagh. He's the biggest landowner round about, and I seem to recall that he is a magistrate to boot.'

'I believe he is. Yes, Raffles, we must

return at once and let him know about this dreadful scheme.'

'As you say.' As he set off, Raffles added thoughtfully, 'But I'm not sure that I should be the one to tell him.'

'Raffles?'

'Oh, he must be told, Bunny, but I think it might be best coming from you.' As I looked a question, he added, 'You see, for various reasons I do not wish to figure too largely in things just at the moment. You follow?'

Of course I did not, and of course I murmured, 'Just so,' or something equally ridiculous. Insofar as I could see a reason for this prevarication, I thought it might be that Raffles was angry with Lord Ardagh on account of the latter's own little ploy, and that my friend did not want to be seen to help the noble earl. Unworthy, I know, but such was the thought that occurred to me, and I sympathized with Raffles for acting that way.

I sought out Lord Ardagh, and stammered out some tale of having overheard a couple of rascals talking. Ardagh seemed sceptical at the outset, but when I spoke of a bomb at the barracks, he took more notice.

'It may be nonsense,' he said, half to himself, 'but I can't afford to ignore even a remote possibility. Thank you, Mr Manders, I shall inform the colonel at once.' And off he went.

The remainder of the day passed somehow or other, the only noteworthy event being a visit from the adjutant of the barracks, with some searching questions for me, where exactly had I overheard the men, had I noticed their appearance, and the like, to all of which I made some halting reply. I could tell that both the captain and Lord Ardagh, who was present at the interview, were sceptical, but as Ardagh had said, they could not afford to ignore my warning altogether.

At dinner I faced similar questions from Lady Alice, and again I had to improvise. I could not face Lord Ardagh and Freddie after dinner, so I pleaded a headache and went to my room. I rather hoped that Raffles would look in to tell me how — if at all — his plans for

Patricia and Charlie were working out, but he did not do so.

* * *

I slept well that night. Or at least I did until the early hours, when a terrific explosion made me shoot bolt upright in bed. There was a hideous grey light filtering through the windows, and when I managed to look properly at my watch I saw that it was around six o'clock.

I struggled out of bed as my door was flung open and Raffles looked in. 'Fun and games downstairs, Bunny!' he called and disappeared.

I threw on a dressing gown and followed Raffles downstairs, to find Lord Ardagh and his wife, Freddie, and the servants gazing ruefully at a large hole in one wall.

'The side door,' said Lord Ardagh briefly. 'Blown off its hinges, and the frame gone, but no other damage as far as we can see. Well, Ellis?' he asked the butler, who had been outside examining the wall.

'A few bricks loose, my lord, but it's mostly just the door gone. No real harm done, thank Heaven.'

'Amen to that.' Lord Ardagh looked at me. 'The conversation you overheard was evidently a plant, Mr Manders, a trick to put us off the right scent. I must say that I was suspicious from the first, it seemed a sight too glib. They evidently knew you were there, and spoke their lines, as the actors say, accordingly, knowing that you would tell me.' He glanced round. 'Here, where's Pat? She's never slept through all this commotion, surely?'

Freddie, Raffles and I exchanged glances, then Freddie raced upstairs, with Raffles and me close behind. Lady Patricia's room was empty, the bed in disarray, and every indication of a hasty departure.

Freddie went downstairs more slowly than he had gone up. 'Pat's gone!' was all he could manage.

'It rather looks as if the intention was not to destroy your house, Lord Ardagh, but to kidnap your daughter,' said Raffles soberly.

'Kidnapped? Pat?'

'It seems that way. For ransom, perhaps, or possibly in the hope of obtaining some political advantage.'

'The devils! Well, if it's money, I'll pay. As for the other thing, I hardly think that my influence is so great.'

'Well, we must wait until they contact you. Unless, that is, we can catch the rogues first,' said Raffles. 'I shall let the local constabulary know, and the colonel.'

'Yes, yes, of course,' said Lord Ardagh, rubbing his head and pretty obviously feeling that he ought to have thought of that. 'Yes, very sensible. Freddie will go with you.'

Raffles and Freddie set off down the drive, but we saw them halt after a score of paces. Freddie turned to face us, waved, shouted something inaudible and ran off down the drive. Raffles merely stood there, looking incredulous.

I cannot say just what any of the rest of us said at this odd behaviour; in any event it was nothing to the flood of surprised utterances that was unleashed a moment later, when we saw Lady Patricia and a young man whom I did not recognize come arm in arm up the drive, with Freddie close behind.

'Pat!' cried Lady Alice. 'What on earth has happened? And you, Mr Moran! What is going on?'

So this was Charlie Moran, I thought! A good enough looking young fellow, as Raffles had said, but with no real light of brilliance in his eye. He and Lady Patricia were speaking together, Lady Patricia saying, 'Oh, it was dreadful!' and Moran explaining that he had been out early on his way to work, when he saw Lady Patricia being dragged along by two villainous looking men. Moran, in his own words, 'waved my walking stick at them and said a few words, and off they ran.'

Lord Ardagh's first concern was naturally to reassure himself that his daughter was unharmed. His next words were for Moran. 'I think that perhaps I have — but then! Well, no real harm's been done there. The police will want to talk to you, of course, Mr Moran, but when that's all taken care of, perhaps you'll come to dinner tonight?'

And of course Moran said he'd be delighted, and shook hands with the earl, and with Raffles, and me. I fancied than I saw a hint of a wink in his eye as he was introduced to Raffles, but I could not be sure, and Raffles' face remained immobile.

There was a good deal more talk than I have set down here, naturally, and most of it centred around Moran and his bravery, and Lady Patricia and her narrow escape. At some point in this discussion, I steered Raffles to one side and looked a question at him. He shrugged, as if to apologize. 'A hackneyed plot, I fear, Bunny. Unworthy even of your talents, but it worked, and that's the main thing.' He passed a hand through his hair, which was much disarranged. 'No time for any niceties this morning, Bunny! I don't think I'll be missed if I go upstairs and repair the damage.' He was gone before I could reply.

I drifted back to the little crowd. Before I could add my voice to the congratulations being heaped upon young Moran, Raffles came flying downstairs, his hair still unbrushed and his dressing gown flapping. 'Wasn't just kidnap!' he gasped out.

'What's that?' asked Lord Ardagh.

'The wretches have taken my gold cuff-links!' said Raffles. 'I expect they've cleaned some of the other rooms out, too, in the confusion!'

Lord Ardagh's face fell. 'My wife's emeralds!' and he flew upstairs, to return a scant moment later, his distraught face telling its own tale.

Lady Alice was, as you may imagine, in need of some consolation. As Lord Ardagh and Lady Patricia went to her aid, Moran frowned at Raffles. Raffles took him aside and spoke in a low tone. I caught odd words here and there, 'Unreliable assistants . . . I could hardly know they would . . . evidently thought we had not paid them sufficient . . . be in Dublin by now . . . '

Moran looked far from satisfied, but was clearly in no position to say anything.

Raffles added, 'In any event, I should have thought that it was a small price to pay for your future happiness. Especially as it isn't you who's being asked to pay it!'

Moran's face cleared. 'By Heaven, you're right, Mr Raffles!' He held out his hand. 'I'll not forget this day's work, I promise you.'

Lord Ardagh did not let the matter rest for long. In an hour we had a visit from an inspector of the Irish Constabulary. He was nobody's fool, that inspector. He told us that the rebels might well have planted other bombs, 'infernal machines,' he called them, in our rooms or our luggage. We would not recognize them, but he would, and it was no trouble to him to take a look, make sure that we were safe, no trouble at all.

He took most time over the possessions of Raffles and myself, saying that it would be a coup for the Fenians to blow up a famous cricketer and his friend. He showed particular interest in Raffles' cricket bag — which went with AJ everywhere — and tapped the base thoughtfully.

'It's a false base,' said Raffles casually. 'I sometimes use it to store valuables and so on. Wish I'd put those gold cuff-links in there, come to that!' And he flipped open the secret compartment, which had so often been used to store our booty, to show that it was empty.

'H'mm,' said the inspector. But he said no more, and he did not try to stop Raffles and myself leaving the next day — earlier than originally planned, but Raffles pointed out that Lord Ardagh would have to commission repairs and so forth, and would not want us hanging around getting underfoot. Ardagh made no objection; I reflected rather sourly that in view of the changed position of Mr Charles Moran, Raffles was no longer a necessity.

One thing puzzled me. 'Well?' I demanded of Raffles, as we sat together in our first class compartment on the quiet little train that was taking us to Belfast.

He sat there, a Sullivan between his lips, tossing a cricket ball idly in his hand. 'Well, Bunny?'

'You know what I mean! Where are they?'

For answer, he threw the ball to me. 'A pretty little device, don't you think?'

I gazed at it. 'Does it unscrew, or something?'

'You have it, Bunny!'

I twisted the ball, which came in two. Inside, nestled in cotton wool, was the Ardagh necklace. 'When did you acquire this? The container, I mean.'

'Oh, a while back. The weight is wrong, of course, when it's empty, but a small handful of gold sovereigns, padded so as not to rattle about, makes up the difference, and I can remove as many or as few as needed when once the swag's in there. I don't know if it's strictly essential, mark you, for even a professional probably wouldn't notice. But I like things to be just so.' He glanced at me, and if I did not know better, I should have said that he was embarrassed. 'By the way, Bunny, there's no need to recount any part of this tale in public, is there? That 'temporary contrivance' business still rankles, you know.'

'I promise to suppress all mention of it, at least until it can no longer matter,' I assured him. As I said earlier, I kept my promise; but when I referred in passing to the episode as a 'dull affair,' Raffles, though approving the adjective, had some harsh words as to the suitability of the noun.

2

ICE COLD

'Cold as Christmas, Bunny,' said AJ Raffles with a shiver, turning away from the window of his flat in the Albany. He lit a cigarette, grimaced and threw it into the fire, for it was very definitely not a Sullivan.

I passed him my cigarette case, which contained my last three specimens of the only brand. 'Things are bound to get better,' I urged him, though truth to tell I had little enough confidence in my own words.

This was in those halcyon days before Raffles' disgrace and my own imprisonment. 'Halcyon' days? Well, we were at liberty, and under no suspicion so far as we knew, but when you had said that you had said everything. The last few months had been a succession of dull days, enlivened by the occasional disaster. My attempts at writing were selling but fitfully, and Raffles, thanks to my timidity, had not 'worked' at his alternative profession for almost half a year. In summer, of course, things had been different, there had been invitations, in which I was included, and life had been relatively easy. In winter, with no cricket, and consequently no invitations — well, matters were getting desperate, and I feared that Raffles would be embroiling me in one of his schemes before too long.

'Did you contact the detective story editor you were chasing?' he asked me. 'The man at 'Criminal Days,' or whatever it's called?'

'Oh, him! He did a bunk. Must have taken his stories too much to heart. Owed his tailor thousands, and his wine merchant even more, so there seems little prospect of my getting my miserable five guineas.'

'I see.' Raffles looked sidelong at me. 'Look here, my Bunny, it is an axiom that desperate times call for desperate measures.'

'Raffles — '

'Meet me here tomorrow and we'll have lunch and talk things over.' And with that he ushered me out, deaf to all my bleats of protest.

What could I do? Raffles was right, of course, desperate action was called for, and that meant only one thing, but for all that I cursed Raffles bitterly in my mind as I walked home through the damp, foggy streets. It was a week before Christmas, but there was little enough prospect of any cheer or goodwill for us, unless we returned to our lawless ways. I had not even the wherewithal to buy a decent Christmas lunch for myself, let alone a present for Raffles.

I was at the Albany the following day, and Raffles greeted me with a rueful look on his face. 'I tried to ring you, but your telephone isn't working,' said he.

'Cut off by the Exchange,' I answered shortly.

'I see. Can I break our appointment?' were his next words.

'Oh, by all means. But why?'

For answer, he waved a note at me. 'I have been asked to lunch, Bunny, and I'm afraid the invitation does not include you this time.'

'One can hardly expect every invitation to include me, Raffles. Anyone I know, though?' I added, curious.

'You'll know the name, if not the man. HHB Morgan.'

'Good Lord!' I did indeed know the name. 'HHB,' or Henry Harrington Barrington Morgan, to give him his full and splendid title, was no relation to the American financial dynasty of the same name, although in his early days he had never bothered to correct the frequently made assumption that he was, an assumption which doubtless did him no harm.

There were those who thought that his name was assumed, deliberately chosen to have echoes of that other Henry Morgan who made himself rather a nuisance on the Spanish Main. Certainly HHB had a piratical reputation in financial circles. No-one quite knew how he had arrived on the London stage, or where his money came from in the early days — gold and diamonds had both been hinted at, though the traders in South African shares denied any knowledge of him — but everyone knew that he now had a controlling interest in the Megalithic Investment Trust Company.

He had been the darling of the City a couple of years ago, although his star was now shining a little less brightly than it had once shone. His reputation for adroitness had become a reputation for ruthlessness, and in fact there were one or two rumours circulating which came under the heading 'libellous.' A friend of mine with some connections in the Square Mile had shown me the last annual report from the Megalithic earlier that year, and shook his head over it. 'It looks to be doing well, and the dividend is up again, but half the investments are unquoted,' said he, 'and I believe that there is a good proportion of the capital which simply isn't listed here at all. Don't tell anyone I said as much, of course,' he added somewhat hastily, 'but although the shares are up, personally I wouldn't touch it with a barge-pole.'

I assured him that I would not — a

promise I could keep without the least difficulty, as my investment portfolio at the time had consisted of five shillings in the Post Office, a sheet of twopenny stamps, and a sovereign on a 33–1 long shot in the Gold Cup.

Such, then, was the man who had invited Raffles to lunch! 'I wonder why?' I mused aloud.

Raffles laughed. 'You don't think he could love me for myself, then, Bunny? Perhaps you are right. Possibly he wants me on the board of the Megalithic, to add a little lustre?'

'There are tales — ' I began.

'I have heard them. You may be sure I shall walk carefully, Bunny. But he should give me a decent lunch, if nothing else, and there may well be something else. I'm only sorry you can't come as well.'

'I'm not! There's sure to be something else, as you put it, and I suspect it will not be entirely to your advantage, Raffles.'

He laughed at this, and assured me again that he would be careful. Then, as it was near the hour of his appointment, he left me, with a promise to meet me at tea time to tell me how things had gone.

I took my own modest luncheon at an ABC teashop, and passed a couple of hours looking at the bright displays in the big department stores. As the last of the daylight faded, and the Christmas lights were switched on, I returned to the Albany, to find Raffles seated at his ease smoking a fat cigar.

'Courtesy of my host,' he told me, passing me another Havana. 'Or perhaps I should say 'our' host, Bunny?'

'Oh? And why that?'

'Because we are invited, you and I both, to pass the Christmas week at Morgan's house in Oxfordshire.'

'Oh,' was all that I could manage at first. Then, 'Why?'

'Ah, there we must enter the realms of speculative philosophy, Bunny. It was, as you may imagine, my own question. His answer? 'Famous cricketer and his friend, lend distinction and perhaps even an air of excitement to the house party', and so on and so forth. All very flattering.'

'But specious?'

Raffles frowned. 'I should be inclined

to think so. I have no illusions, Bunny. We are not invited for ourselves, as a rule, but for our cricket, and there is none at this time of year. Of course, the offer may be genuine, he may wish to impress his other guests. Still — ' and Raffles shrugged his shoulders, and remained indifferent to any further suggestions on my part. 'It should prove interesting, whatever the source of the interest. And he certainly spares no expense when he entertains,' was all he would say.

Despite my reservations, I had no intention of refusing Morgan's invitation, for I knew I should not get another of the kind — or indeed of any kind! A few days later, then, I met Raffles at the station and we travelled together to Oxfordshire.

Whatever the motive for Morgan's invitation, I thought, he did us very well. His carriage was there to meet us, and our rooms were everything that one could wish.

I suppose I have to say that dinner was an interesting enough occasion, although we were not a large party. The other guests were an elderly widow, one Lady

Whitechurch, with her niece and companion, Cynthia; there was the editor of a large and very conservative newspaper and his wife, and a local magistrate and his wife. Cynthia was an attractive girl, and I judged that she had the potential to be lively, in the right company, but she was very much overshadowed by her aunt. Lady Whitechurch and the rest of the guests, by contrast, were anything but lively. Indeed, I have never encountered a duller crowd of people, and I could half believe that Morgan might have wanted Raffles and myself to add a little sparkle to the proceedings. I determined to earn my corn, then, and attempted to engage my neighbours in conversation, only to be rebuffed at every overture. Lady Whitechurch was particularly off-hand with me.

In a somewhat sulky silence, I ate my dinner, which was excellent, and covertly observed the company with a more professional eye. Our host wore a large and ostentatious diamond pin, and another large diamond glittered on his finger. The other men had no jewellery, and I turned to the ladies. Cynthia wore a string of pearls, not very valuable but they suited her complexion; the wives of the newspaper man and the JP both had diamonds, nice enough but nothing special; and Lady Whitechurch had some old emeralds not unworthy of the attention of the lawless individual. But it was Mrs Morgan's necklace which caught my attention and held it all through the meal. I do not know the correct technical term — the word 'scapular' comes to mind, but I cannot remember if it means a style of jewellery or a bone in the human body — in any event, it was a sort of hybrid between a necklace and a Valkyrie's breastplate, some six inches at its deepest, the whole thing being a sort of crescent shape, white gold with the largest and finest diamonds I ever saw, and so many of them, too! I saw Raffles give it a casual glance, then avoid looking again, but he caught my eye and nodded, just slightly.

There was some desultory conversation after dinner, and I managed to get Raffles on one side. 'You saw it?' I asked without preamble.

'One could hardly miss it!' he said laughing.

'Well?'

'Tempting, I allow. But tell me, Bunny, what d'you say to our fellow guests?'

'The drabbest crowd of bores I ever met. Cynthia excepted, of course.'

'Dull, but worthy?'

'I suppose so.' I regarded him suspiciously. 'And — oh! Excellent witnesses, you mean?'

'You surpass yourself, Bunny. Certainly they were not asked for their brilliant conversation. But witnesses to what, I wonder?'

We soon found out. The rest of them very soon excused themselves and went to bed, exactly as one might have predicted. As Raffles and I were about to do the same, Morgan, the only one left in the room apart from ourselves, said, 'Mr Raffles, I should be grateful for a word with you, and — ' with a contemptuous look at me — 'your friend.'

'Ah. I was rather expecting that,' said Raffles.

Morgan raised an eyebrow at this, but

said nothing as he led us to his private study and closed the door. 'You noticed my wife's diamonds?' he asked, without even offering us a drink or a cigarette.

'I thought them rather fine,' agreed Raffles.

'I want you to steal them. Tomorrow will do.'

I think I must have leapt out of my chair, but Raffles never turned a hair. He lit a Sullivan, and said, 'I do not think I heard you correctly, sir.'

'Oh, you heard me all right!' Morgan opened a drawer of his desk, and produced a sheet of paper. 'I've watched your career with some interest, Mr Raffles, and I don't mean your cricket. It is rather odd that many of the house parties you have attended have been blighted with burglaries, is it not?'

Raffles shrugged a shoulder. 'Scotland Yard have thought the same, as I understand it. But they have not thus far insulted me with a direct accusation.'

'Oh, I don't deny that you've been clever,' Morgan conceded. 'I might well have done the same as Scotland Yard, and dismissed it as some monstrous coincidence. But, you see, I have something which Scotland Yard does not have.' And he waved the sheet of paper at us.

'Indeed?'

'Indeed, Mr Raffles. Tell me, does the name — mean anything to you?'

I started again, for the name he mentioned was that of a 'fence,' that is to say a receiver of stolen goods, with whom Raffles had had dealings in the past.

Morgan nodded at me. 'Your friend could do with some of your self-control, Mr Raffles,' he said offensively. 'I think we can drop the pretence.'

'Well, and suppose the name does mean anything?' Raffles nodded at the sheet of paper. 'What does this mysterious person say?'

'Everything, Mr Raffles, everything. Descriptions of the goods you sold him, dates and times, and prices.'

'Let me see if I interpret you correctly,' said Raffles calmly. 'You propose to keep this information to yourself, provided I steal your wife's diamonds?'

Morgan nodded affably. 'Correct in

every particular. If you don't, of course, then this — or not this, for this is merely a copy, the original is in that safe — ' he nodded to a portrait on the wall — 'and I don't think even you will open that, Mr Raffles! — the original, signed, sealed and notarized, will be with the police in a matter of days. In fact, you can keep this copy,' and he threw the sheet of paper to Raffles, who caught it, glanced at it, put a match to it, and flung it, alight, into the large glass ashtray on Morgan's desk.

'But why do you want anyone to steal your wife's necklace?' I asked, puzzled.

It was Raffles who answered. 'Because he's broke,' he said quietly. 'As broke as you or I, Bunny! Broker, if that's the right word. Those nasty rumours in the City are true, then. But he dare not admit it, even to his wife.'

'But why theft?' I persisted. 'Why make a fuss which is sure to involve the police? If I were in your position, I'd have a copy made, and swap the two of them without — ' I broke off, for Morgan had given a guilty start.

'You have such a copy?' asked Raffles.

Morgan started to speak, then got up, moved the picture and fiddled with the safe — making sure we could not see him as he did so — and threw a leather case on the desk. Raffles picked it up and opened it, whistled, and showed me the contents.

'They look real!' was all I could stammer.

'You — !' said Morgan with considerable contempt. 'They ought to, since they cost a small fortune, for all that they're fakes. This is a new process, never been marketed, and it won't be, for I bought up the patents from the — fool who invented it. Only a jeweller, and a good one, could tell the difference.'

'Then why steal the originals?' I persisted. 'Why not just swap them? A lot less fuss and bother, you know.'

Morgan gave a gasp, and looked away in disgust.

'He wants the insurance money, Bunny!' Raffles explained patiently. 'He wants to be paid twice, once by the insurance company, once by the fence to whom he will sell the stones. I shouldn't use — , though,' he told Morgan quite seriously, 'for he will cheat you. And then betray you,' he added, steel in his voice. 'Yes, Bunny. An ingenious enough scheme, if it does smack of greed and avarice. I had better take this,' he said, hefting the fake necklace casually in his hand.

'No, you won't, you — !' and Morgan produced a wicked-looking little revolver, apparently from thin air.

'Consider!' said Raffles earnestly. 'I steal the real necklace — I alone, for I assure you that Bunny here is as pure as the snow now driving against your window — and what will happen? The police will want to search everyone in the house, the innocent and the guilty. They will ask you to open the safe, and lo! The necklace — this necklace, that is, real to all outward appearances — is in there. They will immediately suspect an insurance fraud, and arrest you. You will, I give you my word, be far safer letting me take the fake as well as the real thing.'

Morgan jerked the barrel of the revolver in a menacing fashion. 'Hand it over!' Raffles reluctantly did so, and

Morgan went on, 'All very clever, Mr Raffles, but the police won't search anyone in the house — not even you — for the simple reason that you will make it look as if the thieves came from outside. There have been one or two burglaries in the area just lately — real ones, sheer coincidence, nothing to do with me — and the police will assume that it is the same gang, an assumption which your fellow guests — excellent folk, all — will confirm is correct.'

Raffles nodded. 'I've heard there is a gang at work locally, it's true.'

'Take your time,' said Morgan, 'examine the house tomorrow, and do the job tomorrow night — I suggest when everyone's in bed, my wife is a heavy sleeper, and I won't disturb you if I hear you — but I'll leave the time to your discretion. And I'll leave the other little details, footprints in the snow, jemmied windows, and the rest of it, to you as well. I'm sure you know more about these things than I do,' he added offensively, putting the fake necklace back in the safe. 'And for good measure, if there is any doubt in the minds of the local constabulary, I have the receipts and so on for the copy, and any decent jeweller will confirm that it is a copy. Call me sentimental if you will, but the fake did cost a good deal, and I don't want to part with it.'

'Particularly as it looks so very real?' said Raffles quietly. 'After all, why settle for two payments if you can get three? The average fence wouldn't realize that that's a fake, or not until it's too late.'

Morgan laughed in his face. 'I knew you were the boy! A man after my own heart! A great pity we didn't meet sooner, for we might have worked together.'

Raffles shuddered at the thought. 'Very well, I agree, since I have no choice. You'll give me the run of the house tomorrow, to weigh things up?'

'Of course, as long as you're discreet.'

'And when the job is done, you'll hand over that statement?'

Morgan fairly sneered at him. 'Ah, I do not promise that, not just yet. I do promise that I won't send it to the police, though. You see, it's not altogether out of the question that I may need your specialist services again in the future, and, as you observed, I'm a man who believes in insurance. And I promise you one thing, though, Mr Raffles. Double-cross me, and the police will get that document!' He nodded at the door in silent and contemptuous dismissal.

'We'll say 'good night', then,' said Raffles quietly, and he took my arm and led me out, telling me to be silent when I ventured to express some of what I felt about Mr Morgan.

'What d'you think to our host now, Bunny?' he asked, his eyes sparkling, when we were safely in his room.

I told him. At some length, I fear.

'I tend to concur,' said Raffles when I had stopped from sheer exhaustion. 'He is 'not a very nice man', as my old nurse would say.'

'And mine usually added, 'Come away!',' I said. 'But we can't very well, can we?'

'Not just at the moment.' Raffles lit a cigarette. 'You know, Bunny, those diamonds are the finest I've ever seen! And I mean to have them!'

'Well, then, take Lady Whitechurch's emeralds as well, could you?' I said sceptically. 'I could use some cash myself.'

'You know, I think I might. After all, no self-respecting burglar would take just one item, would he?'

It was said with such assurance that my scepticism vanished. But my awareness of the magnitude of the task did not. 'And the other business? The document?'

'Ah, yes, the document. That does present a problem. But don't you see, Bunny, that the problem of the document is quite different from the problem of the diamonds? In the first place, I'm by no means convinced that Morgan won't send the document to Scotland Yard, even if I do steal his precious necklace, because quite frankly he strikes me as a double-dealing, back-biting yellow cur of the worst sort. And even if he doesn't send it now and give us away, he won't hand it over to us, so what's to stop him calling on our 'services' at any time in the future? For his fortunes are sure to decline again, once the cash from this particular swindle is spent.'

'H'mm, that's true.'

'And I for one don't relish the thoughts of being a sort of hired crook, an unpaid one at that. We're sure to run up against something that we can't and won't do, and then the document will land at Scotland Yard anyway, so it's simply a matter of deferring the inevitable. And then there's the question of the diamonds, Bunny — if we hand them over to Morgan, he'll keep the proceeds without any thought of sharing with us, and we still have our own bills to pay!'

I nodded, but could contribute nothing worthwhile.

Raffles smoked in silence for a moment or two, then went on, 'Bunny, you're a good fellow, but I need to think this out by myself. Cut along to bed, and get a decent night's sleep. And if you could, keep Morgan away as much as possible tomorrow, would you?'

'Away from what?' I asked.

'From me, of course! I'll need to think,

and observe, and I can't do that with him nearby.'

I did as he suggested, and went to bed, but I fear I did not get a decent night's sleep, or anything like it. I felt that we were damned if we did, and damned if we didn't, and I could not honestly see even Raffles coming out of this with any honour, much less any profit.

I saw him only briefly at breakfast, and as I passed him he lowered his voice and said, 'Remember!' The trouble was I did remember, I remembered that that was the last word Charles I said on the scaffold! A bad omen, I thought. In the event I did not have to keep Morgan occupied, for he kept out of the way pretty much all day, I rather suspected in order to avoid any suggestion that he had been seen with Raffles and myself if anything went wrong. And I feared more and more as the day drew slowly and agonizingly to its close that something would go wrong. I tried to get Cynthia on her own, purely to break the monotony, but her wretched aunt insisted on playing gooseberry.

In the afternoon I excused myself from the game of cards that had been set up in the drawing room — 'For fun only, strictly no gambling,' and wouldn't you just know it, in that company? — and set off for a brisk walk to clear my head.

I went over the lawn and through the park, looking for Raffles but not seeing him anywhere, until I found a little wood with some farmland beyond. I was delighted to spot a hare, obviously as bored as I was myself, gambolling about in the snow, all on his own, perhaps getting into training for the boxing matches he would have with his rivals in love in a few weeks time. I stood there entranced for a quarter of an hour, and was startled when Raffles' voice whispered in my ear, 'All Bunnies together, eh?'

'A hare, Raffles, not a rabbit. And where the devil have you been anyway?'

'Oh,' he said vaguely, 'getting the feel of the place, the lie of the land.'

'And have you formed any plan, then?'

'An outline, my Bunny, an outline. It will need courage, though, and not a little luck. Has Morgan been obtrusive today?'

'Rather the reverse. I think he's avoiding us, in case — you know.'

'I do indeed. Look here, can you try to keep him away from me this evening, if necessary?'

'Naturally. And is that all?'

He nodded. 'You had best not appear in this at all, Bunny. Just in case.'

'I hardly think so!'

He gripped my arm. 'Bunny, your courage is not, and never has been, in question. Don't you see I need a man on the outside, in case of emergency? Your main task is to keep Morgan out of my hair, but also to be ready to use your initiative.'

'Put like that, of course — '

'Good man! And now it is almost time for tea.'

We returned to the house, but as soon as we entered, Raffles excused himself and vanished. I realized almost at once that he was starting his 'plan,' and in answer to a question from one of the others as to where he was, I made some non-committal reply. He came into the room ten minutes after tea had been served, full of apologies for his lateness, and telling a charming story of having stopped longer than he had intended to watch a hare playing in the snow!

After tea Raffles pleaded a headache, and vanished once more. There was no general movement to follow him upstairs, for it was that curious time that you get only in winter, when tea is over but it is too early to think of changing for dinner, and all you want to do is sit in your armchair and gaze at the ever-darkening sky.

It was fully dark, and people were starting to light lamps here and there, and there was a shuffling as we thought of dinner and the attendant preparations, before Raffles turned up again. 'Hello!' I said. 'Feeling better?'

'Yes, thanks. I had fallen asleep, but I fancied I heard — ' Raffles was standing by the door, having just come in. The rest of us had turned to look at him, as you do when someone enters the room, but as he broke off his sentence and stared down the room at the French window, we all turned back again to follow his gaze, and were astounded to see the window standing open, and just inside it two large men, both wearing black masks over their faces, and both holding revolvers.

I cannot remember who said what. Someone said, 'Damn!' and one of the ladies let out a little scream, all very understandable in the circumstances, but mostly we just stood or sat where we were, too surprised to do anything.

One of the men said, 'Stay where you are and you won't get hurt,' which was hardly original, but I suppose there is a set form for these things, and we stayed where we were accordingly, which is what he wanted. The speaker, evidently the leading light in the team, told his mate, 'Keep 'em covered, while I get the stuff,' and made his way out past Raffles, obviously making for the bedrooms.

'This is deuced awkward,' said Raffles, half to himself.

I stared at him, wondering if he had somehow arranged the whole thing himself. Was this part of his plan? I had not seen him all day, he could easily have gone into the village, a mile away, and sent a telegram or something. Only his face, a comical mixture of disbelief and chagrin, gave me pause. He caught me looking at him, shrugged, and laughed, much to the amazement of everyone else in the room.

After a very short while, as it seemed to me, there were heavy footsteps outside. The door flew open, and the burglar who had gone upstairs started into the room, pretty clearly in a bad temper. His way was blocked by Raffles, who spoke to him in a low voice. I was nearest to them, and fancied I heard Raffles say some such phrase as 'something to your advantage,' but I could not be certain. I am certain that the burglar hesitated a moment, then motioned with his revolver to Raffles to step out into the corridor. The two of them were out there no more than a minute, then they returned, Raffles first, and the burglar, his good humour obviously restored, following.

'Anyone who steps outside in the next ten minutes will be shot,' the burglar informed us, and then he, and his still silent confederate, made their way out through the French window.

'Telephone the police at once!' shouted Morgan to anyone who would listen.

'I think they will have cut the wires,' said Raffles calmly, and this proved to be the truth.

Morgan's next suggestion was that someone — Raffles, me, the JP, the editor, the butler — should follow, for, as he said, 'The - - - won't be out there! They've made good their escape by now! It was an empty threat! There's not the slightest danger!'

'In that case,' said the editor, speaking for the first time in my presence since I had been introduced to him, 'in that case, why don't you go out there yourself?'

Morgan subsided at that. But only for a moment, and then he demanded angrily of Raffles, 'What the devil did you say to that chap?'

'Oh,' said Raffles easily, 'I merely said that since he had Mrs Morgan's diamonds — that was what they came for, of course — there was no need to bother with things like our cuff-links and signet rings. It would waste some considerable time, and they are really worth so little.' Morgan snorted angrily at this, but Raffles went on just as calmly as ever, 'And I persuaded him to leave Miss Cynthia's pearls with me,' and he produced the string from his pocket and handed it to her.

'Thank you, Mr Raffles! They're not valuable, I know, but they were my mother's.' And she put them round her lovely neck.

'And now,' said Raffles cheerfully, 'I think the rest of you should check your belongings. They have the diamonds, and I strongly suspect they have Lady Whitechurch's emeralds — catch her, someone!' he added, as the lady fainted on hearing this — 'but I couldn't say what else they might have taken.'

Morgan made a gurgling noise and rushed out, returning a moment later to gasp, 'The - - - -s have rifled the safe!'

'Only to be expected,' said Raffles, adding casually, 'Anything valuable gone?'

Morgan choked, and turned purple.

After ten minutes — and ten minutes seems an awfully long time under those circumstances — we did go outside, and of course the crooks were long gone. Then the butler had to go into the village for the local constable, who had to telephone the sergeant, who had to call Scotland Yard. I think there is no need to describe the comings and goings, the questions and answers. The police seemed convinced that the two men were that gang which had committed the other robberies round about, and none of us seemed disposed to contradict that view.

It was not until the early hours of the morning that anyone managed to think about bed. I pushed Raffles into his room, and shut the door firmly. 'What did go on between you and that burglar chap?' I asked him. 'Was he part of your plan?'

'Do you suspect that I lied, then?'

I looked for a weapon, but found only Raffles' silver-backed hairbrush. 'I could mark you with this, though,' I told him.

He laughed, and lit a cigarette. 'Well, then. No, he and his mate were most definitely not part of my plan. In fact, I was never more startled in my life than when they walked through that French window! As for what I said, I simply told him that I knew he had not found Mrs Morgan's diamonds.'

'Oh? And — '

'I knew that,' he said patiently, 'because of course I had taken them myself, about ten minutes earlier.'

'Oh!'

'I confessed my crime, but said that rather than face exposure and social ruin I would surrender my spoils.'

'And you did?'

'Oh, yes. But I really did ask him to leave Miss Cynthia's pearls, and he agreed. Said he'd only taken them because there was nothing else remotely of value upstairs or in the safe.'

'So he did crack the safe? I thought that might have been you! He must have recognized the fake for what it was then, which is logical, I suppose, him being an expert as it were.' I caught Raffles' cynical eye upon me as I burbled on, and asked, 'Wait, though

— what about the emeralds? Did he not take those?'

'I took those at the same time as I took the diamonds, of course. Be sensible, Bunny!'

'And you still have the emeralds?'

'Oh, yes. The burglars didn't know about those, you see, it was the Morgan diamonds they were after.'

'Well, we have something out of it,' I said grudgingly. 'A pity you had to hand the diamonds over!'

'Bunny, my Bunny! I did not hand the diamonds over, as you so engagingly put it.'

'No? But — '

'I handed over the fakes, which I had taken from the safe even earlier today. Morgan rather over-rated the difficulty of opening the safe, by the way.'

I was still puzzled. 'But I thought you said the crooks had opened the safe?'

'They did, the second time. And found it empty, as I had already taken the fakes.'

'And the incriminating document?'

'If you examine my grate,' said Raffles nodding at the fire, 'you may find traces of its ashes, though I doubt it.'

'I confess I am not entirely with you, Raffles. Just what was your plan?'

He sighed. 'I had made some preparations during the day. I borrowed some boots from the hall cupboard, and made some very convincing tracks in the snow. I then jemmied a side window, which the police did not notice, since of course they knew the thieves had come and gone through the French window. Just before tea, I opened the safe and I took the fake necklace, and the document, from it, leaving the empty jewel case.'

'Yes. Why? I mean, I can see why you took the document, but why the fake diamonds?'

'To give to Morgan, of course. Don't interrupt. When I had finished my tea, I said I had a headache. I went upstairs and took the real diamonds, and Lady Whitechurch's emeralds. Now, I had intended to place the real stones in the safe — '

'Good Lord!'

'Well, can you think of a safer place? No pun intended. You see, Bunny, I did not share Morgan's touching faith in the police being fooled by the scheme he had concocted. I fully expected the police to search everyone here, and thoroughly at that. The police would perhaps not examine the safe, but if they did do so, and the real stones — not to speak of the Whitechurch emeralds — were in the safe, then Morgan would prove they were fakes and all would be well. If he failed to prove that, or failed to explain the emeralds, then it would be Morgan whom the police arrested, for fraud, robbery, or what-not, and not us. If, as I thought likely, the police did not check the safe, then all would be well. I intended to give the fake necklace — which I planned to put in a temporary hiding place when people went upstairs — to Morgan, and I imagined that he would put it straight in the safe.'

'Wouldn't he see the real stones?'

'The theft would be detected about the time I handed the fakes to Morgan, and there would be the devil of a fuss, so I did not think he would examine them too closely. But then I had also planned to put the real diamonds in the empty jewel case. The safe was full of papers, and I planned to bury the emeralds under those. Of course, if he went through the safe — and opened the jewel case — then he would be sure to see them, but they would not be obvious to a casual glance, and I could not believe that Morgan would stand there going through the safe, and jewel case, with us in the room, even if the theft were not discovered! He might look at the supposed fakes when I handed them over, and even compare them in his mind with the supposed real diamonds, but what of that? He would see minor differences, if he saw any, but that would only make him more convinced of the quality of the fakes! Even if he opened the jewel case, so what? After all, he would expect to see two sets of diamonds in the safe, and that is what he would see. But as I read it, he would lock the safe immediately the fakes were back inside it, and try not to mention its very existence to the police, try to forget he had a safe, until the fuss had died down, for he dared not risk its being searched by the police.

And that was all I wanted. All I needed was for the stones to be undetected for a few hours, as long as the police were in the house, in fact.'

'But I still don't see the point! All you would have done was to ensure that the fake diamonds, and the real diamonds, and the emeralds, were all together in the safe, instead of just the fake diamonds!'

'Ah, but I never intended to leave them in there! I planned to return at my leisure, when the police had left, having searched the place — and us — and proved us guiltless. I confess that when I took the real diamonds I toyed with the notion of leaving Mrs M the fakes in their place, but I dismissed the idea. With the document gone, Morgan would know that I had been into his safe anyway. And then I did not want him to have even the consolation of selling the fakes for what he could get! And for good measure, I had an idea the fakes might prove useful in the future. A pity I had to hand them over to that burglar chap, but it really could not be helped, Bunny!'

My head was spinning — not for the

first time in my acquaintance with Raffles. 'I begin to see your plan. And Morgan could hardly complain that the jewels — real or fake — had gone, not when the theft had already been investigated and he had claimed the insurance money!'

'You read my mind, Bunny. And with that incriminating document gone, we were safe. Of course, my plan was but half complete. I went downstairs with the real diamonds, the fake diamonds, and the emeralds, all variously disposed about my person! I planned to put in an appearance, then when people went up to change for dinner, I would put the real stones in the safe, and the fakes somewhere else. But it was then that things went awry, or seemed to, because it was then that those crooks — and I swear they were nothing to do with me — appeared. As I say, I foisted them off with the fakes.'

'But the real stones? You had not put them in the safe, you say? Incidentally, Raffles, I think I might have improved upon your plan! I should have taken the real stones first, and made only one visit to the safe instead of two!'

Raffles laughed. 'You give me more credit — and less — than I deserve! I was making the 'plan' up more or less as I went along, you see. It was largely a matter of timing. I could not go upstairs for the real jewels until everyone came down for tea — but I could open the safe. And the main thing, the vital thing, was that damned document! Jewels or no jewels, I had to have that document, Bunny! As I said, I toyed with the idea of leaving the fakes, and only settled on leaving the real stones in the safe at the last minute. There was simply no time, my Bunny. I still had the stones, the fake and the real, in my pockets. And come to that, excepting the fakes, I still have!' And with that, he drew diamonds from his left pocket, and emeralds from his right.

I put a hand to my forehead. 'Suppose the police had searched us?'

Raffles laughed. 'And why should they, when everyone had seen the crooks make off through the French windows? For all that, Bunny, I am happy that it was not our old friend Inspector Mackenzie whom Scotland Yard sent. He would have insisted on searching us, I fancy! And that would have been the end. Still, all's well that ends well, Bunny.'

Not for the first time during our short stay, I slept badly, and Inspector Mackenzie, our old adversary, found his flatfooted way into my dreams. I was pleased when the hour of our departure came, the other guests had left a little before, but Raffles seemed in no great hurry. In vain I urged haste, but he merely smiled and said 'All in good time.'

And then — just as we were about to leave the house, Morgan came in, that damned little revolver pointed at us again!

'Oh, really!' said Raffles with a sigh.

'If you would?' Morgan gestured with the barrel, and we moved into the billiard room, to be greeted by none other than Mackenzie himself, and a couple of his associates!

'You're not leaving without being searched,' Morgan told us.

'I have no objection to Inspector Mackenzie searching me,' said Raffles in a bored tone, 'but I refuse to have you present.'

Morgan blustered, but Mackenzie backed Raffles, somewhat to my surprise, and our erstwhile host had to leave.

I confess I was trembling, though Raffles, as always, was serene and untroubled. How could he be so calm, I asked myself, with the diamonds and emeralds concealed about him? Mackenzie did search us, and downright thoroughly, to the very skin, but without success. It was the turn of our luggage next, and I trembled anew, and with increased vigour. The stones must be found now! Still, at least the personal search was over, and I had been able to put my trousers back on before we were arrested!

But Mackenzie found nothing. He emptied our bags, searched our meagre belongings, examined the linings of the bags, even emptied Raffles' tobacco pouch, all to no avail.

'Well,' said Mackenzie, obviously as baffled as I was myself, 'I'm very sorry, gentlemen, but Mr — ' he emphasized the word — 'Mr Morgan insisted, and my superiors listen to him.'

'For the moment?' suggested Raffles quietly.

'Ah, we have our eye on him, I'll not deny it. There are stories, you know. Just a little bit of proof, that would be enough for me. But getting that bit of proof, that's another matter.'

Mackenzie and his merry men escorted us to the station — 'Just for the look of it,' as Mackenzie said — and we all travelled back to London together, Mackenzie growing philosophical as he smoked some of Raffles' tobacco, and telling us that it was very likely the same gang that had committed the other robberies in the neighbourhood.

'I dare say you're right,' said Raffles. 'Look here, Mr Mac, you and I have had our differences, I'll not deny it, but if you had a Bible about you, I'd swear here and now that I have nothing to do with those two burglars. No man in that room was more startled than I when they appeared.'

'I'll testify to that!' I said without thinking.

Mackenzie laughed. 'I don't dispute it,' said he, and we parted the best of friends.

I returned to the Albany with Raffles, in no very happy mood, despite our having evaded Mackenzie's grasp. 'I don't know how you knew we'd be searched, though!' I said, when we were alone.

'Oh, I told you that I mistrusted Morgan. I did not expect Mackenzie, though, I'll grant you that. However, I did fully expect Morgan to hold us up and search us, for I knew that he thought the burglary a put-up job, and so I got rid of the stones.'

'A pity, Raffles! It will be a miserable Christmas, now! Still, we had a decent dinner, though the company wasn't very congenial. Better than porridge in a police cell! And it was a good breakfast.'

'Yes, I noticed you stoking up on the kippers, Bunny. Perhaps just a light lunch?'

'It'll be all light lunches, and dinners too, unless any of my editors are feeling generous!'

'My treat,' said Raffles. 'But nothing to drink, mind.'

'Oh?'

'We need clear heads for tonight, and our return to Oxfordshire.'

I stared at him.

'Bunny, Bunny! I know you are not the quickest of men, but you are inordinately slow just now. I mean to burgle Morgan's safe, of course.'

'But — oh! That's where you hid the jewels?'

'Last night, when all the little rabbits — and snakes — were asleep. As I say, I did not trust Morgan an inch.'

'But suppose he checks the safe?'

'I do not think he will, for he knows, or thinks, rather, that there is nothing of value left in it. But suppose he does? I hardly think that he will inform his wife, and Lady Whitechurch, and his insurers, that all is well, do you? No, he will be puzzled, no doubt of that, he'll wonder just what the devil has been going on — but he'll be delighted, too. And I fancy his delight, and his greed, will far outweigh his puzzlement. He will leave the stones where they are. Oh, he may think it as well to move them as soon as possible, lest we — or our business rivals — return, but it is the holiday season, and besides, he dare not take them openly to the bank. No, he will leave them where they are, in the unlikely event that he discovers them. In any case, I don't think he will expect us to return so soon!'

In the event, our return visit was something of an anti-climax. We lurked in the shrubbery until the last light had been extinguished, then broke in, using the side window that Raffles had jemmied the previous evening — the butler had evidently not thought it worth bolting the stable door, so to speak — opened the safe, and took the stones, which were, Raffles whispered, quite undisturbed. We did ten miles in a little over two hours, and caught a workman's train at five in the morning at a little wayside halt.

After breakfast, Raffles vanished with the stones, to return after lunch with a satisfied smile on his face.

'All done?' I asked.

'In the bank, Bunny, metaphorically and literally. I'll give you a cheque for your share in a moment.'

'I trust you didn't use - - - -?' I said laughing, naming the man who had betrayed us to Morgan.

Raffles frowned. 'Certainly not. I had all but forgotten him. I wonder how best he should be handled? Perhaps — ' He broke off and gazed at the door of his bedroom. Putting a finger to his lips, he stood up and started towards the door, only to stop in his tracks as it was opened.

Our old friend, the senior burglar, stepped into the room. He wore his mask, but there could be no mistaking either him, or the small, wicked-looking revolver he pointed at us.

'Another small but wicked-looking revolver, Bunny!' sighed Raffles. 'Are people giving them as Christmas presents this year, I wonder?'

Our uninvited guest placed the revolver on a table. 'To establish my good faith, gents,' he said, with an awkward little bow.

Raffles picked up the gun, glanced at it, and handed it back. 'It is duly established,' he said.

The burglar put the gun in one pocket,

and took a chamois leather bag from another. 'We were both done!' he said shortly, throwing the bag to Raffles.

Raffles took out the necklace — the fake, of course — and examined it closely before passing it to me. 'Bunny?'

'Fakes?' I said, putting what surprise I could into the word — I suspect it sounded authentic, for by this time I had but the sketchiest notion of what might be going on. 'They are very lifelike.'

'Too — true!' said our guest. 'I was fooled, but my fence wasn't. You can have that as a souvenir, if you like.' And he turned to go.

'One moment,' said Raffles. 'I happen to know that the man from whom you — we — took these stones has claimed from his insurers as if they were genuine. Honest crooks I don't mind, but fraud is another thing altogether.' He picked up pen and paper. 'I happen to know the firm is the Northern Midland, and I think, yes — 'The enclosed, the subject of a claim against you by HHB Morgan, Esq, and which came recently into my hands, may interest you'. That will suffice,

I imagine, for insurers are astute men. A cardboard box, a little brown paper — so! I'll post that tomorrow.'

'I'll do it on my way home,' offered our guest. 'There are such things as postmarks, you know.'

'That is very civil of you,' said Raffles. 'And you really had no need to go to so much trouble. Perhaps this will compensate you somewhat — ' and a rustle of banknotes completed the sentence.

'You're a good 'un!' said our guest with admiration.

'Before you go, the fence who rejected the stones was not by any chance . . . was it?' and he mentioned our betrayer.

'Not — likely! Only a — fool 'ud trust 'im!'

'I trusted him,' said Raffles quietly, 'and he betrayed me to my enemy.'

'Did he, now?'

'I was not after those stones by accident, nor yet of my own accord. It was suggested to me that I steal them.'

'I see.'

'And where a man betrays once, he can easily do so again. It occurred to me that perhaps some of — 's friends might care to have a word with him, show him the error of his ways?'

'Yes, I — his friends, I mean — might just do that small thing.' Our guest nodded, and let himself out, presumably via the window through which he had entered.

'You were not quite honest, you know, Raffles,' I said. 'You as much as suggested that — told you to steal the stones, not Morgan.'

'Oh? Did I really give that impression? The two are well matched, Bunny, and they both deserve whatever is coming to them.'

'And another thing, Raffles — that burglar chap knows who we are! You, at any rate. How on earth did he know that? And aren't you afraid he will use that knowledge against us, at some time?'

Raffles shrugged. 'As to who we are, he probably made enquiries of the butler, or somebody, in the local pub. Assuming the butler was not in on the robbery, of course, and that wouldn't surprise me in the least! Betray us? I hardly think so,

Bunny. Didn't you see his face when I mentioned . . . and his betrayal of us? Honour among thieves, Bunny, that's the watchword,' And he lit another Sullivan, and laughed at my expression.

The insurers were interested in the fake necklace, very interested indeed. They called in Scotland Yard, and Mackenzie himself arrested Morgan for insurance fraud. The day after the news of the arrest broke, the shares in the Megalithic Trust began to slide; when trading resumed after the holiday the dealings in the shares were suspended; ten days into the new year the firm went bust, and Mackenzie's investigation was widened to include all Morgan's business dealings. And, at the spring Assizes, Morgan was sentenced to ten years in the Dartmoor quarries.

The 'fence' who had betrayed Raffles simply disappeared. I gather that the police view was that he had feared their attentions, and had left the country to escape detection, but I rather fancy that the squalid alleys and rotting wharfs by the London River could tell a different tale.

All was not unrelieved gloom and despondency, though. Raffles and I — and the unknown burglar, too, I have no doubt — had a very Merry Christmas, and a prosperous start to the New Year.

3

RAFFLES AND MISS MORRIS

'Work?' asked AJ Raffles incredulously. 'Work?'

'I only suggest it as — '

'My dear Bunny, your own literary efforts, enchanting, vivacious, and so on, that they may very well be, have so far singularly failed to earn the recognition they indubitably deserve. As for my own poor abilities — well, when you say 'work' to me, Bunny, it means only one thing!'

'Oh, Lord!' I gazed at him miserably.

Raffles shrugged his shoulders, and looked out of the window of his flat in the Albany. It was early spring, but the balmy days, the feathery green plumes on the plane trees, the girls in their new dresses, all these were wasted upon us just then. The proceeds of the Morgan jewel robbery had long been spent, and we having, in Raffles' own words, 'to think again.'

'Anyway,' said he, turning back to me, 'come along and I'll buy you lunch.'

'Can't, I'm afraid, though I appreciate the offer. I promised to go and have a drink with a chap. You could come along with me, if you like?'

Raffles shook his head. 'I need to do some heavy thinking, Bunny, and I know how your glass or two at lunch time can so easily degenerate into a debauch worthy of Tiberius or Caligula.'

I left him still staring out of the window, and a feeling of foreboding crept over me as I made my way outside, for I knew well enough what sort of heavy thinking he would be doing.

It does not matter just where I went, or what the name of my friend might have been, but what does matter is a remark that friend made as we stood together at the bar. We were both bemoaning the parlous state of our finances, and he laughed and said, 'I could wish that I had some skill as a detective, you know!'

'And why that?' I asked, all but spilling

my drink — for my conscience makes me extravagantly sensitive to any mention of police or detectives or anything of that kind.

'Oh,' he said, 'I hear that old Morris is looking for a discreet agent to investigate the disappearance of his daughter.'

I frowned. 'Gustav Morris? Mildred Morris?' This Morris, I hardly need remind you, was the founder, sole proprietor, and general presiding genius of Morris & Co., the gigantic department store in Knightsbridge. Mildred, his only child, was an attractive but, by all accounts, a scatterbrained girl whose portrait and exploits appeared regularly in the illustrated papers. 'Has she disappeared, then? I hadn't heard anything of the kind.'

'It hasn't been made public, of course.'

'Then how do you know about it?' I wondered.

'Some of the chaps were talking.'

'Oh, if it's only gossip — !'

'More than gossip, old man, more than gossip,' my friend assured me, patting my arm earnestly to reinforce the point. 'You know what the newspapers say — 'we are reliably informed', that kind of thing. Apparently old Morris is frothing at the mouth. Offered a huge reward.'

'Oh?'

'Yes, hundreds. Thousands, very likely.'

'But you don't have a precise figure?' I asked sceptically.

'No,' said he very seriously, 'as I told you, it hasn't been officially announced, so to speak. But it stands to reason, doesn't it? A chap like that, rich as Croesus, only daughter, and what have you? Bound to offer a reward. Attractive girl, too,' he added, producing the latest issue of the 'Strand' magazine and turning to the 'Society Beauties' page.

'I have seen her picture more than once,' said I, glancing at the page. An idea, or the germ of an idea, at any rate, was starting to form somewhere at the back of my mind. 'Look here,' I said, waving the paper, 'd'you mind if I borrow this?'

'Oh, keep it,' he said.

'Thanks, and I'll see you later.'

'Oh, are you off?' and he stared after

me as I practically ran from the place and set off back to the Albany.

I found Raffles still contemplating the view from his window, and smoking his Sullivans. I told him what I had been told, and showed him the 'Strand'. 'Well?' I demanded.

'Very nice, Bunny.'

'Yes, she's an attractive girl. But what about — '

'Not the girl, Bunny, though she is, as you say, not too hard to look upon. No, I was meaning those,' and he tapped a finger against the diamonds which circled the neck of Miss Mildred Morris.

'Raffles, how can you think of jewels at a time like this?'

'It's my trade, Bunny, and you must allow a man to be proud of his trade. Did Jack Falstaff not say something of the sort? But you're right, my Bunny. The father must be worried if the daughter has indeed vanished. A reward, you say?'

'So Rumour has it.'

'Ah, Rumour of a Thousand Tongues! Well, it would be only natural, would it not? I must say, the whole business has been kept very quiet, assuming for a moment that Rumour mistakes not the truth. I had heard nothing of it, I must say. Still, it might be fun to play the policeman's part for once, might it not, Bunny? Yes, here's another of those 'Sherlock Holmes' stories in the 'Strand'.' He glanced at the paper again, and laughed. 'Not that I think he'll last, Bunny! Too much the inspired amateur for my taste. No, I don't think you or I would have anything to fear from Mr Holmes.' He took his stick and coat from the rack. 'Pass my hat, would you, there's a good chap?'

'Shall we see Mr Morris, then?'

'We shall indeed.' Raffles took the latest 'Who's Who', the Bible of his 'trade,' from his shelf, and consulted it. 'Fashionable town address, of course. Come along, Bunny.'

Mr Morris's town address was in the most fashionable part of Mayfair, and I quailed at the basilisk gaze of the butler who admitted us and took our cards. But Raffles never turned a hair, and greeted Mr Morris, who came out to see us, with a cheery 'Hullo!' and a firm handshake.

Morris was somewhat under the middle height, perhaps fifty years of age, but his hair was still untouched by grey, and his eyes were wonderfully penetrating. He showed some signs of fatigue, which made me suspect that the rumours were not far short of the mark. His first words confirmed this. 'Mr Raffles, I have heard of you, of course. And your friend,' he added with a rather patronizing nod in my general direction. 'But you must excuse me, sir, for I am rather busy just at the moment. I would not like to be unhospitable, but pray be brief.'

'It is about your daughter, sir.'

Quite unexpectedly, Morris's attitude changed. His face darkened, and he took a step towards Raffles. 'If you're a friend of that damned rascal — ' he began.

The butler, who had been lurking in the background, hastily moved to block his master's way; I stood in front of Raffles, bleating, 'I say!' or something equally ineffectual.

Raffles himself never moved or spoke until things had calmed down a little, then he raised a hand, and told Morris, 'I assure you, sir, that my motives in coming here are purely to lend you whatever assistance I might. I know nothing of this matter save what gossip tells me.'

Morris subsided a little at this. He dismissed the butler with a nod, and waved us into what was evidently his study. 'I suppose it was only to be expected that word of this would get out,' he said in an undertone, helping himself to brandy with a slightly unsteady hand. 'Would you care for anything?' he asked as an afterthought, waving the decanter.

'A brandy would be very acceptable!' I said.

Raffles frowned at me. 'Nothing for either of us, thank you,' he said firmly. 'We wish to keep clear heads for this very serious matter.'

'Of course.' Morris hesitated. 'I hardly know where to begin,' he said ruefully.

'Well, to begin with, are these stories true? Has your daughter disappeared?' asked Raffles.

'Not disappeared in the literal sense, inasmuch as I know, in broad terms, where she is. And with whom,' Morris added gloomily.

'Has she been abducted, then?' I asked.

'Not in the conventional sense, sir.'

'Run off, then?'

Morris winced at my words. 'You put the matter very baldly, sir, but you are not far from the truth.' He swigged his brandy, shuddered, and went on, 'Last year, my daughter took a holiday at Biarritz. Business commitments meant that I could not go with her, but I made sure that she was accompanied by a most respectable lady who acted as a chaperon. My daughter is, I regret to say, somewhat headstrong. She eluded the watchful eye of her guardian more than once and, as she puts it, 'had some fun' on her own account. On one of these pleasurable and illicit excursions, she made the acquaintance of a man whom I personally would not care to know, a man named Pargetter, if that indeed is his real name. A glib and good-looking rogue. A gigolo, if you want the plain word, gentlemen.

'Well, she had to return to London, of course, and did. And this fellow stayed over there. But then, three weeks ago, no more, he turns up here in London, having apparently taken a house somewhere in the city, though I do not know the exact address. Now, I have told you what happened — or what I assume happened — but I was myself in utter ignorance of all this until the occasion, three weeks back, when this fellow turned up here, left his card! Then, of course, my daughter had to tell me some of what had gone on, though I had to read between the lines quite considerably.' He paused, and took a more measured pull at his brandy.

'I take it that you were not favourably impressed by the young man?' Raffles asked.

Morris snorted. 'I was not, sir! Indeed, once I saw what was going on, I forbade him to come here again. My daughter, who is, as I told you, of a temperamental nature, flared up at this, said she would not be treated like a child, the usual things. And then, two days ago, she left me a note saying she was going to stay with this fellow until they can get a licence and be married!'

'I say!' I gasped.

Morris waved a hand. 'It is not quite so bad as it might sound, for there are servants in the house, a housekeeper who is, I trust, quite respectable, and who can chaperon my daughter. But still, the situation is far from satisfactory.'

'Your objection to this man is a personal one?' asked Raffles.

'Personal, sir. And financial.'

'Ah!'

Morris hesitated, then said, 'My late wife was a wealthy woman in her own right. When she died some eight years ago, she left a fortune in trust for Mildred. A fortune, gentlemen, and I use the word advisedly! When my daughter should come of age, she was to have the income from the money, and she has drawn that income now for two years, for she is now three-and-twenty. But if she married, being of age, she was to have the entire capital as well, to do with as she chose.'

'I see,' mused Raffles. 'A fortune, you say?'

'A positive fortune, sir.' Morris shrugged.

'I have no financial interest myself, of course, since I have a claim neither to interest nor to capital. Nor, frankly, do I need it. But I should hate to see this ruffian get his hands on the money.' If ever I heard a man speak the truth, it was then. Morris was evidently one of those men who derive pleasure not merely from the accumulation of wealth for themselves but from the denying of it to others. Although, to be honest, I could see that he had a point in the present instance.

Raffles was saying, 'I may be able to help.'

'I should, of course, be most grateful.' Morris hesitated. 'A modest reward, some slight recompense, would not be altogether inappropriate. A hundred, shall we say?'

'A hundred? To have your daughter back, out of the hands of an unscrupulous rogue?' It was wrong of me, I know, but I could not keep the words back.

Morris flushed. 'Five hundred, then! I'm damned if I'll haggle! Five hundred, when my daughter is returned to me.'

'With no questions asked?' said Raffles.

'No questions asked. I don't care how you do it.'

'Agreed.'

A flurry of handshakes sealed the bargain, and before I knew it Raffles and I were outside in the street.

'What a charming fellow, Raffles!'

'He is not too prepossessing, is he, Bunny? But one must make allowances.'

'And have you a plan?'

'A vague idea only. The first problem is to find where the lady is staying.'

'It could be anywhere, though!'

'Hardly, Bunny. If this fellow is in effect a confidence trickster, then he must act in a fashion calculated to build his victim's confidence, must he not? That means a decent house in a stylish location. It should not be too difficult to find out if anyone arrived from Biarritz three weeks ago and took such a property.'

He was right, as always. At the third house agents we tried, we found the address we sought, and went there at once. It was, just as Raffles had predicted, a large house in a reasonably desirable neighbourhood. We kept a lengthy watch from a convenient doorway opposite, avoiding the glance of a passing policeman, and were rewarded by the sight of two young people who emerged, escorted by a large and fierce-looking woman, towards the hour when honest folk are setting off for their dinner.

Miss Morris was even lovelier than her picture; her male companion was a year or so older than her, and good looking in what I must call a coarse sort of way. All did not seem sweetness and light, though; as they climbed into the carriage I heard Miss Morris speak rather sharply to Pargetter, and he tried to laugh it off and made but a poor show of it.

'His face is his fortune, Bunny,' said Raffles, echoing my unspoken thoughts.

'Yes. Lord Ardagh could have made use of him!'

'Bunny!' Raffles frowned at me, then turned his attention back to Pargetter. 'Though I expect he'll go to seed once he reaches thirty, as all these fellows do. Damned if I couldn't take to him myself, were I that way inclined!'

'Really, Raffles!'

'A professional assessment only, my dear fellow.'

Something was nagging at me. 'You know, Raffles, I could swear I've seen that fellow somewhere before.'

He shrugged his shoulders. 'A common enough type, Bunny. So, they're off to their dinner. Now, I wonder? Should we go to ours, or should we act tonight?'

'Tonight?'

'This very night, Bunny. The problem, you see, is one of time, or the lack thereof. This fellow wants to get his hands on the money, and to do that he has to marry the lady. So he'll want to do that as soon as possible, and that means he'll be wanting a special licence, or whatever it's called. Can't say that I know the technical details, or would want to, but one gathers that these things can be speeded up by special dispensation. And there seemed a slight difference of opinion there, did you notice? If the lady is having second thoughts, Pargetter will want the ring on her finger as soon as possible, so that it's too late for her to change her mind.'

A horrid thought struck me. 'Suppose

they're married already?'

'H'mm. I rather think not. If they were, then Mr Morris would have heard from the gentleman's solicitors regarding the cash. And besides, would they go out to dinner on their wedding night? And if they did, would they bother with a chaperon? I think not, on balance.'

'And your plan?'

'Ah, my plan. It involves our providing ourselves with masks and revolvers, and getting into that house.'

'Raffles!'

'Nothing like that, Bunny, I do assure you.'

'Raffles, I've had occasion to speak rather harshly to you more than once about your secretive nature. Will you tell me what you propose?'

He regarded me for a while, then laughed. 'You are right,' he said. 'Very well then, Bunny. It's no good our taking the lady from the house and returning her to her father by force. She's of age, she would simply go back to her lover. Nor it is any use trying to tell her what sort of a man he is, for she wouldn't listen. Her father has already tried, and she didn't listen to him, so why would she listen to us, complete strangers?'

'He — '

Raffles held up a hand. 'The only thing to be done, the only thing that has a ghost of a chance of working the trick, is to show her what sort of a man he is. To make him reveal his true nature. And that's what I intend to do.'

'Raffles — '

'Does that satisfy you? Any points on which you would desire further clarification?'

'No, that's fine, as far as it goes. But Raffles, what I was trying to say was, suppose he isn't a villain, after all? Suppose old Mr Morris is seeing things through a father's eyes, quite understandably, of course, but blinkered, so to speak? Suppose this Pargetter's intentions are honourable, after all?'

Raffles thought a moment. 'I confess, Bunny, that the prospect had simply not occurred to me. But now you mention it, my little plan should allow for that too. Yes, Bunny, we'll see this fellow in his true colours tonight, and if those colours are clear and — oh, be damned to this metaphor, for I don't even know if it is artistic or nautical! If he's a regular chap, we'll find that out tonight, Bunny, and if so then he's welcome to the girl, and Morris may go to the devil, and there's an end to it!'

We secured the masks and our revolvers, though we did not load these, Raffles saying that the precaution was unnecessary. We returned to the house, donned our masks, and entered via a rear window, one of those absurdly ineffectively fastened and so very convenient rear windows which make the burglar's task so easy! A moral here for the honest householder, note! We made our way to the drawing room and concealed ourselves behind the heavy curtains.

'Now, Bunny,' Raffles whispered, 'I suspect they'll come in here, but if not we shall track them down. If they do come in here, I'll do what's necessary, and you will remain under cover until I call you.'

'As usual!'

'Bunny, how often must I tell you how important is your task? If I am not much mistaken, then we have to deal with a thorough-going villain, and I may be in very real danger tonight, danger from which I rely upon you to extricate me.' And with that, unsatisfactory though it was, I had to be content.

We lurked behind those curtains for an hour, two hours, three, then Raffles gripped my arm. 'Ready, Bunny?'

I heard the door open and the sound of lamps being lit. Raffles had his eye to the slit of the curtains, but I had to be satisfied with listening to events unfold in the drawing room.

'Here we are!' The voice of the man, Pargetter. Educated, or pretending to be educated? It was hard to tell. There was a sort of subdued giggle, presumably from Miss Morris, then Pargetter said, 'Thank you, Mrs Green, that will be all.' I took it that Mrs Green was the companion, or housekeeper, or something, who had accompanied them. Whoever she might have been, she was evidently in no hurry to leave, perhaps feeling that it was not entirely proper to leave the two of them alone in there, a sentiment with which I heartily concurred — I mean, I would have concurred with it had that been Mrs Green's sentiment, if you follow me.

It was not until a young woman, presumably Miss Morris, said, 'It will be fine, dear Mrs Green,' that an older woman's voice said, 'Good night, miss,' adding reluctantly as it seemed to me, 'Sir,' and there were sounds of footsteps leaving the room and the door closing.

'Well, here we are,' said Pargetter again. 'Just the two of us.'

'Not quite.' It was Raffles who spoke, in his best East End accent, as he stepped out into the room, waving his revolver in an easygoing fashion. 'Don't make no noise, lady, and nobody'll get 'urt,' he added. 'It's them sparklers I'm 'ere for, nothink else.'

I was now able to shift myself a foot or so towards the slit in the curtains, and could now see, as well as hear, what was happening.

'You cur!' It was Pargetter who said it, and in a surprisingly firm voice, as he stepped between Raffles and Miss Morris. 'If you want that necklace, you'll have to deal with me first!'

'I will,' promised Raffles. 'Move yourself, or so 'elp me, I'll shoot!'

'You won't shoot!' Pargetter's words had the ring of certainty. 'You haven't got the nerve. Clear off, before I thrash you! And where's your pal, come to that? I know there must be another of you somewhere, you haven't the courage to work alone.'

I shuddered. Had Pargetter, or one of his creatures, seen us enter the house? Was he so very confident because he knew he faced an empty pistol? It seemed rankly impossible that he should know, but yet I could not account for his attitude in any other way. Unless he were braver than any man I have ever known, brave to the point of foolhardiness.

Raffles was facing the two young people, and his back was to the door. But from my hiding place I commanded a view of the entire room, with only a slight movement of my eyes, and to my horror I saw the door being opened, slowly and

111

carefully. Miss Morris and Pargetter saw it too, I could tell that. Miss Morris gasped, but Raffles must have taken that as being part of her general distress, and ignored it. Pargetter never turned a hair, to do him credit, but remained as cool as Raffles himself.

What could I do? Raffles had told me to remain in hiding until he needed me. And it certainly seemed as if he might need me, for two men, masked like Raffles and myself, armed with revolvers like Raffles and myself, made their way into the room!

Raffles, of course, was still watching Pargetter, who was talking in the same blustering fashion, calling Raffles all sorts of a coward, and daring him to do his worst. The first Raffles knew of the two newcomers was when one of them shoved his pistol into Raffles' ribs, and said hoarsely, 'Stick 'em up!'

Raffles did not move for a moment, then he laid his revolver on a little table.

Pargetter's reaction was odd. It is true that he asked, 'Just what is going on?' but I swear he was unafraid, almost as if he knew exactly what was happening. He sounded almost, were it not ridiculous to think it, amused by the turn events had taken!

The burglar who had his gun in Raffles' ribs said, 'Yus, what the ---- is going on?'

'I dunno,' said Raffles, still in character. 'Nothink to do wiv me, these two geezers.' He jerked a thumb at the newcomers.

Pargetter's face never changed as he said, 'You mean — what do you mean? Two gangs of crooks?' Again, that odd note was in his voice, a note which betokened some special knowledge, or I missed my guess.

I stepped out from the curtains. In my best Limehouse tones I said, 'I don't know what they mean, but I mean to shoot the first one as moves! Put them guns down, you two!'

Raffles gave me as grateful a look as any man can manage who is wearing a black silk mask, as he recovered his own weapon and took the pistols from the two burglars, who were clearly puzzled. 'This is a pretty kettle o' fish, I must say!' he told me.

'Yus, what they calls a 'cow inside ants', I think.'

His look of gratitude was replaced by something less sympathetic. 'Coincidence be damned!' he said. 'Somethink's wrong 'ere, and I want to find out what.' He jerked the barrel of his revolver in a menacing fashion at the nearest burglar, who flinched.

'Don't shoot! I'll tell yer!'

'Go on, then,' urged Raffles.

'It was 'im, wasn't it?'

''Im?'

''Im.' The burglar indicated Pargetter, whose face had changed — indeed, he was now looking positively unwell. ''E told us you'd be 'ere. Paid us to stick you up, and then make as if to fake a burglary, like, and then run off when 'e defended the lady 'ere'.

'You unspeakable wretch!' It was neither Raffles nor I who said it, but Miss Morris.

'But why'd 'e do that?' asked Raffles, barely maintaining his accent in his astonishment.

'Oh, I can tell you that!' said Miss

114

Morris. 'This villain persuaded me to leave my home and my father and fly with him! I confess I was not entirely unwilling, but then some doubts crept in, doubts as to the advisability of my actions, and doubts, I will be blunt, as to this man's ultimate intentions. He sensed that, and has concocted this ridiculous scheme to convince me that I should admire him — and marry him! Well, it has failed, sir,' she told Pargetter, who slumped into a chair. 'If these — gentlemen,' she indicated Raffles and myself, and the pause was barely perceptible — 'will be so kind as to escort me home, then I shall leave you to settle accounts with your hirelings there.'

'O' course, lady. Just get yer coat an' 'at, won't yer, and we'll be orf.' And whilst Miss Morris made her preparations, Raffles took the two supposed 'burglars' to one side, and tore off their masks. 'Now,' he told them, 'you don't know me, but I knows you! An' if ever you mentions this little affair — ' and he waved his revolver in a menacing fashion.

We escorted Miss Morris back home. It

was no great distance, I am pleased to say, for Raffles and I dared not take a cab nor yet remove our masks, so we had to walk. Fortunately Miss Morris was so angry with her former paramour that she did not remark upon our informal progress, nor yet our odd costume. We left her at the gate, and she flounced up the drive, with her thanks unspoken.

'There's gratitude for you!' said Raffles. 'And I didn't even take her necklace! By the way, Bunny, what the devil was your accent supposed to be?'

'East End, Raffles! I was rather proud of it.'

'East End? More like the West Riding of Yorkshire!'

'Well, yours was nothing special! It would never 'ave passed in 'Oxton, guv'nor!'

'I assure you, Bunny, I have made a careful study of phonetics! But I rue not taking that necklace, old chap!'

'There's always the reward,' I told him. 'We could hardly claim that, had we lifted the necklace! And Morris knows us, remember, he'd be sure to want the

116

blasted thing back.'

'Ah, yes, the reward, to be sure.' And Raffles laughed out loud as he removed his mask.

We were at the Morris house next morning bright and early, but Mr Morris did not rush to receive us. On the contrary, he kept us waiting a full half hour before we were shown into his study. Raffles did not seem at all put out by this, but strolled casually about the drawing room whilst we waited, staring out into the street, or studying the bell pull. At last, the butler escorted us into Morris's presence.

Our host did not seem over eager to see us, and his bearing, too, was not quite what one might have hoped for, or indeed expected, considering the circumstances. 'Well?' was his greeting.

Raffles raised an eyebrow. 'Your daughter is safe and well, I trust?'

'She is, sir. And what of it?'

'We had an agreement, as I recall. A matter of five hundred pounds, and no questions asked — '

Morris snorted. 'I don't know how you

know she's back,' he told us, 'but I don't see what it has to do with you! My daughter has told me what occurred last night,' he went on, 'and it is clear that you had no hand in the matter. 'You can hardly claim the credit for the fact that two common criminals showed some spark of decency!'

'Can I not?' Raffles seemed puzzled.

'Can you?'

I have seldom seen Raffles at a loss for words, but I saw it then. 'No,' he agreed reluctantly, 'I cannot.'

'Then there's no more to be said. You know the way out.'

I stood upon the pavement, furious. 'Nothing irritates a man like being slung out on his ear, Raffles!' I said angrily. 'And just lately, it seems to be becoming a habit! Can you beat that for sheer nerve, though? Fancy his refusing us the reward like that!'

'Bunny, Bunny, calm yourself, dear chap!' And he laughed to himself in an odd, silent fashion. 'I never thought he would pay up, you know.'

'You didn't?'

'A mean man, Bunny, mean of spirit as well as in the conventional sense. It would, naturally, have been very nice if he had paid up, a bonus, so to speak, but I did not expect it. No, dear Bunny, 'twas not the reward I sought.'

'Wasn't it? Then — '

'Bunny, Bunny! I wanted to see the layout of the house, of course! You have probably been so busy studying the pictures of the daughter that you have not noticed any mention of the father's little hobby. He collects gems, Bunny. Not any gems, mark you, but antique carved gems. 'Multum in parvo', if I remember the tag correctly. A lot of value, in a small compass. And he keeps them in the house! You noticed the safe, of course? In his study, behind that large painting of the well nourished and entirely shameless young lady?'

'Oh, so that was it!'

We returned to the Albany, and sat in silence for a while, Raffles smoking his Sullivan. Then a thought struck me. 'Raffles?'

'Yes, Bunny?'

'How long have you had your eye on this gemstone collection?'

He blew out a plume of smoke, shrugged his shoulders. 'Oh, I don't know — some time now.'

'Some considerable time?'

'A year or so.'

A few minutes passed in silence. 'Raffles?'

'Yes?'

'Weren't you in Biarritz last year?'

'Was I?'

'Yes, you were! I say, Raffles?'

'Yes?'

'I told you I thought I recognized that Pargetter fellow?'

'Did you?'

'Raffles?'

'Well?'

'This whole business wasn't some elaborate scheme of yours, was it? Designed expressly to give you an excuse to get into Morris's house?'

'Upon my soul, Bunny!' Raffles laughed, and threw the end of his Sullivan into the fire. 'You give me more credit than I deserve, old chap.'

'Yes, but it might have been.'

'Oh, anything might have been — '

'Yes,' I went on, warming to my hypothesis. 'That Biarritz business! And I thought I'd seen that fellow before! I said as much, Raffles! I've seen him with you somewhere, or I'm much mistaken!'

'Most of my friends look very similar.'

'And the scheme to show him up, get Miss Morris to show her gratitude, ask us into the house — '

'Well, then,' he interrupted scornfully, 'why should I need the second lot of supposed burglars? They were redundant, Bunny. And then Pargetter did not immediately play the coward's part, did he? He was quite calm and collected.'

'Yes, that's true enough — no! Of course, it would look far more impressive if there were three men, in two separate gangs, and Pargetter, or whatever his real name is, seemed full of bravado to begin with and then broke down, which is exactly what he did! Yes, the contrast would be that much more pointed! And it would be a most curious coincidence had you both come up with the same scheme, your staging a fake robbery to show him up for a coward, and then his staging another one to prove himself a hero! A bit much to swallow, Raffles, even for me!'

Raffles lit another Sullivan. 'There is yet another possibility, Bunny.'

I stared at him. 'Is there?'

'Well, suppose for one moment that I had, as you suggest, engineered an elaborate scheme, asked a — friend — to gain the lady's affections and what not. What — just 'what', Bunny, nothing more, 'what if' — what if the man upon whom I had relied to give a convincing impersonation of a coward had, instead, decided to double-cross me, to bring in his own men, to cut me out, prove himself to the lady, and thereby get his hands upon her entire fortune, instead of being content with the miserable pittance I had — might have — paid him? What then? Why,' he went on as I floundered for words, 'who could I ultimately rely upon but my little Bunny, lurking as always behind the arras?'

I put a hand to my head, which was swirling. 'But — is that what it was? But, Raffles — if those two crooks were Pargetter's men, and if they expected to have to deal with you — '

'Yes, Bunny?'

'Their guns were very probably loaded! And mine was empty!' I sat down rather heavily.

He gazed at me sympathetically. 'Ah, but if matters were as we have postulated, they wouldn't expect you, would they, Bunny? They might have been told that I was effectively unarmed, but they would have to work on the assumption that you were not. They would very probably assume that I had taken the same sort of elementary precaution which they themselves would take. And Pargetter could hardly tell them that you were harmless — for one thing, he could not be sure, and for another, it would give the game away to Miss Morris. Once we had their weapons, of course, all was well in any event.'

'Even so!'

Raffles shook his head. 'Let's just say it

worked out rather well, shall we? Yes, I mean to have those gems, Bunny.'

And he did too, though that, as they say, is another story altogether.

4

A CHANGE OF DIRECTION

We were strolling across Westminster Bridge, AJ Raffles and I, at about two o'clock of a chilly and slightly misty Sunday morning in late September. Do not think, dear reader, that we had been engaged upon one of those lawless nocturnal expeditions with which we were, unhappily, all too familiar. It is quite true that our fortunes were at a low ebb, for we had not undertaken any criminal enterprise recently, and over the past few days I had noted the old familiar gleam in Raffles' eye, a gleam which denoted that he had some skulduggery in mind. But any larceny at that particular moment was merely prospective. Despite the lateness — or earliness, if you like — of the hour, we walked in all innocence, with consciences clear as the proverbial crystal, having attended one of those social functions which all men are called upon to attend at some time. It matters not where, or what, it was, and in fact the honest members of the organization concerned would not be too happy if I named it!

We had dined well, Raffles and I, aye, and drunk a little more than was strictly good for us. Or at any rate I had, for Raffles was as abstemious as ever, and his steady hand gave me some much-needed support as I stumbled over a badly laid paving stone or two.

'Never a cab when you need one!' complained Raffles, looking the length of the bridge.

'Who needs a cab, Raffles? Not feeling well, Raffles, old chap? Now, me, I never felt better, Raffles.' And I slapped him heartily on the back. 'Mind you, Raffles, now you mention it, things are a bit quiet, aren't they? Getting late, I suppose, eh, Raffles? In fact, Raffles, we seem to have London pretty much to ourselves just at the moment, Raffles. All London to ourselves.'

'Indeed, Bunny.'

'Apart from that chap there,' I added, nodding to where a dim figure lurked in an angle of the parapet.

'H'mm.' Raffles glanced where I indicated, then took my arm firmly and steered me along. As we passed the man, for a man it was, whom I had seen, Raffles nodded a greeting, and I mumbled some absurd nonsense or the other. The man never answered us, though. Instead, he seemed to shrink into himself, as it were, to squeeze yet further into the masonry of the bridge.

We had gone perhaps another ten feet, and I was muttering something about churlish fellows who wouldn't pass the time of day with a chap, when Raffles slowed down.

'I don't like this, Bunny,' he said. 'I don't like it one little bit. If I didn't know better — yes, by Heaven! Quick, Bunny, or the poor devil will jump!'

And before I had fully grasped his meaning, he raced back to the angle of the bridge, and I saw that the man who had lurked there was now clambering up on to the edge of the parapet, clearly intended to leap into Father Thames rolling sluggishly below.

I ran after Raffles, who had grabbed the man's legs, and was trying to pull him back to the pavement — a dangerous enough task, for had the man been larger and heavier, I am certain they would both have gone over the parapet. As it was, the man was no great size, and Raffles was able to hold him steady until I arrived and lent a hand to pull him back to earth. Once there, he collapsed into a heap, and I had a strong suspicion that he was sobbing.

I confess that I did not know quite how to proceed, for this was not the usual ending to a convivial evening; and Raffles, for once in his life, seemed as much at a loss as I was. I think that Raffles said something like, 'There, there,' and I asked 'What's wrong?' or something of that kind. But before we could get any sense out of the would-be suicide, there was heavy footfall upon the pavement, and we looked up to see a large police constable bearing down on us.

'Cabs and policemen!' groaned Raffles under his breath. 'Never there when you need 'em, but when you don't — !'

The policeman stopped, and regarded the three of us with a sardonic and questioning eye. He did not exactly say, 'Hullo, hullo, hullo!' but you could see that the words trembled, as it were, upon his lips. In any event, the traditional question, 'And what's all this?' hung unspoken in the air.

Raffles straightened up, and took the policeman's arm in a neighbourly fashion. He moved a few paces away, and spoke in a low tone. I caught a few words, 'Modest celebration . . . drop too much . . . uneven pavement . . . find a cab . . . ' And, as he said the last words, a cab did roll past, as if sent by a kindly providence, and Raffles hailed it with unaffected relief. 'If you would, officer?' and we all helped our new friend into the cab.

Raffles thanked the policeman, and I saw a glint of gold. Raffles' good honest face and the good honest coin of the realm together dispelled any lingering doubts the policeman might have felt, and he suffered us to leave without further enquiry.

In the cab, Raffles and I very naturally turned our attention to the dismal wretch we had rescued from a watery grave. He was not, as I had at first imagined, a tramp, an outcast who had decided that he could not face another night on an Embankment bench. He was, in fact, quite respectable in a sort of seedy middle-class fashion. An assistant in an old established gentleman's outfitters, perhaps, or a stock-broker's clerk in a small way of business, one of those nameless, faceless millions who struggle to keep their heads above water in the great metropolis, that was how he struck me at a second glance. We tried to cheer him up somewhat, and succeeded in establishing that his name was Herbert Stourton.

'Well, Mr Stourton,' said Raffles, 'and how do you come to — to be out so late of a Saturday night?'

Stourton gave a sort of shrug of his shoulders. 'I'm sure it's very kind of you to take an interest,' he muttered at last, 'but since you — well, since you met me, as it were, I must get home.'

'Oh?' Raffles raised an eyebrow at this sudden change of plan, and even I realized that it was a curious response in one who had seemed so very keen on making away with himself.

'Yes,' Stourton went on, 'you see, I left — well, a note.'

'Ah! Explaining what you were going to do? And why?'

'Oh, no! Not why! Except in very general terms, of course, the disgrace, and what have you. You understand, I'm sure.'

'As yet, you have not told us anything to help us understand,' Raffles pointed out gently. 'Perhaps it would be as well if we moved from the general to the particular. No,' he went on as Stourton seemed inclined to take him at his word then and there, 'let us wait until we are safe inside.'

'You are very kind, gentlemen. Must get home, though!'

'Oh, very well.' And Raffles passed on to the driver the address, in an unfashionable suburb, which Stourton mentioned. We drove in silence for fifteen or twenty minutes, then the cab drew up outside a very ordinary looking house.

'Will you come in?' asked Stourton, fumbling with his key.

Raffles glanced up at the dark windows. 'Won't we rather disturb your family?'

'Oh, not a bit of it. The wife's at her sister's, and the children. Violet — that's the wife, of course — has been wanting to visit her sister, and this seemed as good a time as any to pack her off, what with — one thing and another.' Stourton unlocked the door, and ushered us inside. 'Find a seat, anywhere,' he offered. 'There's no fire, I didn't want to light one, not to leave it burning when I — well.'

We found seats, and sat there wrapped in our overcoats. Stourton offered us a 'burgundy type' wine, which Raffles refused, though I did not. Raffles himself lit one of his Sullivans, I unearthed a cigar which I had purloined earlier that evening from our erstwhile host — old habits die hard — while Stourton, with a mumbled apology, filled an ancient briar pipe with cheap tobacco. 'Now, Mr Stourton,' said Raffles, 'you were telling us about your little difficulty? But first, there is the matter of this note.'

'Ah, yes, the note.' Stourton went to the mantel shelf, found an envelope there, and put a match to it. We watched as it flared up in the empty grate. Stourton heaved a sigh of relief. 'Not that it matters much, though!' he muttered, quickly growing morose again.

'Your wife had no idea of what you planned?' asked Raffles curiously.

Stourton shook his head. 'I said I would spend the evening with my brother, and that I might well stay the night there. I thought it best to — well, not to worry her too much.'

'Very considerate!' I said with a sneer. 'And what about when she found the note, eh? Wouldn't that upset her?'

'Now, now!' Raffles chided me. To Stourton he said gently, 'You have not been yourself, sir, that much is clear. Tell us what it is that troubles you, and we shall see if we cannot think of a way out of the difficulty.'

'You are very kind, gentlemen,' said Stourton with a sigh. 'But Violet and the children will find out soon enough what the trouble is! And then — I just don't know what they'll do! Oh, why did you stop me, back there?'

Raffles patted his shoulder, and I made some silly remark or the other designed to comfort him. 'If you could begin at the beginning?' prompted Raffles.

'Very well. But I warn you that it's a sordid tale, and I wouldn't be surprised if you're up and out into the street before I've done.'

'I doubt that!' said Raffles. 'We're not easily shocked, Bun — that is, my friend — and I.'

'Indeed not!' I added fervently, thinking of some of our exploits, and realizing that Raffles had deliberately avoided using even my nickname. I think the precaution was probably unnecessary, for Stourton seemed too absorbed in his own troubles to notice what we were saying, though I took Raffles' point.

'Well, then. Don't say I didn't warn you. You see,' said Stourton, 'I work in a pawnbroker's shop. Jameson's, the name is, I dare say you know it? No? Well, old

Jameson, he's not a bad chap, bit rough spoken, but a heart of gold, as they say. Anyway, he has an aversion to banks, you see. Keeps all his money in the safe in the shop.'

'Ah!' said Raffles.

'I see you've worked it out, sir,' said Stourton, sighing again, louder and longer this time. 'Things were going badly with us, you see, gents. The youngest was sick, and we needed a doctor, and how to pay the bills?'

'You helped yourself to a little something?' Raffles suggested.

Stourton nodded. 'I was frightened to death,' he said frankly. 'So scared I didn't dare take more than a couple of sovereigns. But a pal of mine had a tip on a horse, and I thought, might as well be hung for a sheep as a lamb, and so I backed the thing.'

'And it lost, I suppose?' I said.

'No, sir. That's the thing. It won, and my two sovereigns turned into five. It seemed so easy, you see.'

'So you took a little more?' I asked.

Stourton nodded. 'I got interested in

racing, something I'd never taken any particular notice of before. Read all the tips in the papers, and what have you. It all seemed so easy,' he repeated in a dreamy tone. 'Before I knew what was happening, I was helping myself on a regular basis, as you might say.'

'And how long has this been going on?' asked Raffles.

'Oh, about six months.'

'Did your employer not spot any discrepancy?' asked Raffles.

'No, sir. That's what made it so easy. He's not what you'd call a trusting sort of chap, not in the ordinary sense, but he has this great big safe, and he keeps the only key to it — '

'Ah!'

'And so he thinks that it's quite safe, you see.'

'Safe in the safe?' I suggested, but neither Raffles nor Stourton seemed to appreciate this. 'So he never bothers to check?' I added hastily.

Stourton nodded. 'That's right, sir. That is, it was right. But just recently he must have started to suspect something, for he's been dropping hints. 'Time I had a proper audit', and 'Must check the safe sometime', and all that sort of thing. And there was a piece in the paper just last week, a man who'd pinched a few quid from his employer because his wife was sick — the man's wife, not the employer's, I mean — and the employer had refused to prosecute. 'Catch me letting him off like that!' old Jameson told me, with a leer. 'Just as well you've not been helping yourself, eh, Stourton!' I nearly fainted at that! Well, matters came to a head yesterday. Mr Jameson told me that he plans to check the safe this Tuesday.'

'Why did he give you warning, I wonder?' I asked, puzzled.

Stourton managed the ghost of a smile. 'I think he suspects, as I say, and he wants me to have a fair chance to replace the cash.'

'But you can't, of course?' said Raffles.

'No, sir. I can't.' Stourton gave an odd twisted grin.

'Well,' said I. 'Let's see, if you took a fiver a week for six months, that's five sixes, thirty, times four for the weeks, that's — well, say a hundred and fifty. Not a fortune. Of course, it's a hundred and fifty more than I happen to have about me, but I wouldn't have thought — '

'Pardon me, sir, but it's a good deal more than that,' said Stourton.

'Oh? And how much more, then?'

'About three thousand.'

'Three — !' I scattered ash from my cigar over the threadbare carpet, and spilled what was left my burgundy in my agitation.

Even Raffles seemed a touch nonplussed at this. 'I had not quite realized that your misdeeds were on so Herculean a scale,' he murmured. 'Of course, I see your difficulty now. You could never hope to raise that sort of money in a day or so — '

'Begging your pardon again, sir,' Stourton told him, 'but I've got the money!'

'Oh?' I could tell that Raffles had not expected this. Nor, for that matter, had I.

Stourton nodded. 'The horses didn't lose, you see, sir. They won, or most of 'em did at any rate. Of course, I didn't win very much, because the secret is to back the favourites, nine times out of ten, and they're evens, or odds-on. It's a mug's game backing outsiders at long odds.'

'True enough!' I said, wincing at the memory of a thirty to one disaster earlier that day — or the previous day, if we are to be accurate.

'And then I dared not risk big bets, even though I was winning steadily,' said Stourton. 'I feared to lose the lot, you see.'

'But still' said Raffles, 'three thousand! I wonder that your employer did not notice the void in the safe just at a casual glance, never mind bothering to count it.'

'Oh, there's twice that amount in there. Or there should be, that is to say. What remains is enough for day-to-day business purposes. Yes,' Stourton went on, 'I made a decent profit. Nothing spectacular, as I say, and I had the doctor's bills and all, as I told you, and of course that ate up most of my winnings. But I have the money I took, every penny, in cash, and a few pounds over, that's safe in the savings bank, the little bit of profit, I mean.'

We stared at him in silence for a long moment. Then a thought struck me. I leaned forward, hands on my knees, and looked earnestly at Stourton. 'Mr Stourton,' I told him, 'I think I see a way out of your difficulty!'

'Oh?'

'Yes, indeed! You can simply replace the money in the safe!' And I leaned back, triumphant.

Stourton did not react to this brilliance as I had expected. He shook his head, then placed it in his hands. I stared at Raffles. 'Well? Why not?'

'He has already said that he cannot replace the money,' said Raffles gently. 'However, I confess I can see no flaw in your scheme. Mr Stourton, if you have the money, what is the difficulty?'

Stourton looked up. 'The money is is gold,' he said, and replaced his head in his hands.

I frowned. Raffles put a hand in his pocket and took out a rouleau of sovereigns, those little paper rolls in which the bank issue them. 'The last of their honourable line!' he told me, throwing the little parcel to me. 'There are ten in there.'

'I know that well enough!'

'Well, then. Imagine ten times that, there would be a hundred sovs. And then ten times that, and three times that?'

I placed the rouleau on the table, and drew an outline with my fingers, trying to picture three thousand jimmy o'goblins in gold. 'A fair old expanse of coin.'

'And a fair old weight.'

'You see,' said Stourton in a tone of despair. 'The sheer bulk, the volume or whatever you call it? It's impossible! I'd never be able to smuggle it back in! And especially when old Jameson is so suspicious! He'll be watching me like a hawk! Has been, this last week or so. I should never have taken so much! I was greedy, stupid! I should have replaced a few each day when once I started to win, and played only with my own winnings.'

'Ah, but why not replace a few each day now?' I wanted to know.

'By Tuesday?' Stourton did not trouble to hide his contempt.

I subsided. 'Sorry. Forgot it has to be by Tuesday.'

'But there may still be a way,' said Raffles thoughtfully. 'You say you have the money here?'

Stourton nodded.

'Could you fetch it?' asked Raffles.

Stourton stared at him for a long moment, then nodded, stood up, and left the room.

'Raffles?'

He waved an impatient hand at me. 'After all, Bunny, we have cracked plenty of cribs to take money out! I'm glad that you had sense enough not to mention my name, by the way. Continue in that same vein, if you would.'

Before I could think of any reply, Stourton was back, carrying a large leather hatbox, which was obviously of considerable weight.

'Yes,' said Raffles thoughtfully, 'I see the difficulty. Not the sort of thing one could take in and out unnoticed.' He gazed at Stourton. 'Look here, Mr Stourton, I'll make you a sporting proposition. You give that hatbox to me, and my friend here, and we'll get the money back. How does that sound?'

'But I've told you there's a safe!' Stourton fairly gasped. 'How could you hope — '

'Let us say we know men who might be persuaded to help,' said Raffles.

'You'd really put it back for me? In time for Tuesday?'

Raffles nodded. 'Of course, you'll have to trust us. I mean, there's absolutely nothing to prevent our taking the cash and simply spending it, without actually doing anything that might help you.'

Stourton gave a shrug of despair. 'I don't see that it matters very much, if I'm to be honest, gents. If the money isn't back by Tuesday, I've had it anyway!'

My head was starting to clear properly by this time, and I felt it was time I contributed something to the discussion. 'Mr Stourton,' I told him, 'you could simply go to this — Jameson, is it? — and admit the whole thing. Just give him his money back.'

Another shrug was the answer to this. It was Raffles who said, 'That has something to recommend it, but there is an obvious flaw. This chap, Jameson, would naturally wish to make an example of Mr Stourton here, to discourage anyone else from thinking that he was a soft touch.'

'You have it, sir!' agreed Stourton. 'I tell you, even if I admitted the whole thing, and returned the cash, he'll prosecute. I have no doubts as to that.'

Raffles stood up. 'Then there is no alternative,' he said calmly. 'If I might just have a note of Mr Jameson's business address?' Stourton supplied the information. 'And does he sleep on the premises?' Raffles went on.

'Yes, sir, but he's a heavy sleeper, or so he always says.'

'Servants?'

'An old housekeeper, sir. She sleeps most of the day, so I take it she's none too alert at night.'

'Capital! Well, Mr Stourton, I think that will be all.' He nodded to the hatbox, then to me. 'Would you, old chap?'

I do not know if you have ever had occasion to carry some three thousand gold sovereigns about with you? If not, take my word that it is no easy task. By the time we had walked down a couple of streets and found a cab, I was positively staggering under my burden.

Once back at Raffles' rooms, I deposited the hatbox with a sigh of relief. 'What is it you intend?' I asked Raffles.

'Now? Some sleep, Bunny!' He nodded to the couch. 'You can stay here, if you don't mind roughing it. Or would you rather get home?'

'I'll stay, thanks.' It was now a little after three, and I had had enough. But Raffles had not properly answered my question. 'You really intend to replace the money?'

'Oh, yes. As I said, it will be a novelty!' He yawned. 'Good night, Bunny. Don't make too much row if you're up first, will you?'

Needless to say it was Raffles who woke me much later that day. We had a late breakfast, then strolled round to get the lie of the land, specifically the land around Mr Jameson's establishment. The front of the shop was quite hopeless. An iron grille with a great padlock protected the heavy oak door; bad enough in itself, but there was a street lamp right bang next to the shop! Raffles led me to the end of the road, and into a narrower lane behind the shop. This looked more like it. There was a stout door, true, but no grille shielded it; above all, there would be the blessed cloak of darkness under which to do our work.

'It's not getting in,' mused Raffles. 'It's the safe. If it's halfway decent, it'll take time to open, and I don't like the notion of the chap sleeping on top of it, so to speak. Still, there's no other way, so it must be done. This time.' And before I could ask the meaning of his last remark, he took my arm and we strolled back to the Albany.

'Is it to be tonight?' I asked.

Raffles lit a Sullivan and nodded. 'It will be a little quieter, I hope, being Sunday. And besides, I wouldn't put it past this Jameson character to jump the gun and check the safe tomorrow!'

'Raffles?'

'Yes?'

'Why does Stourton's fate bother you?'

'Oh, you know, Bunny,' he said vaguely.

'This miserable worm I tread upon, in mortal whatnot suffers a pain as great as when a giant dies.'

'A quotation, Raffles?'

'As good as, Bunny. Anyway, I haven't opened a lock in ages, other than with a key. I need the practice, Bunny, for unless your literary talents are recognized very quickly, we shall need to work in earnest, my boy!'

Raffles was able in some way to put all thoughts of future lawlessness out of his mind and relax completely, but I had could not. I wandered about Raffles' flat, smoking far to much, but not daring to take a drink. I tried to read the latest weekly papers, I even tried to rough out an idea for a story of my own, though it seemed paltry and contrived by comparison with this scheme on which I was now engaged. And I thought, not merely about the consequences of failure, the court, the prison, the disgrace, but about just why Raffles was helping the wretched Stourton. For I dismissed the notion that Raffles needed any practice in opening a safe! Pity, perhaps? Fellow-feeling for a miserable worm upon whom unkindly Fate had played a cruel trick? I could think of no better reason, unsatisfactory though that one was, and gave it up. Finally, I settled down on Raffles' couch, and tried to rest, though I had little expectation that I would be able to do so.

'Wake up, you lazy devil!' It was Raffles' voice, mocking me.

'Wasn't asleep, Raffles! Merely resting, preparing myself for the fray.' I glanced out of the window, to see that it was already pitch dark. 'Are we starting now?'

He nodded, and we set off. I had that damnable hatbox again, and Raffles had a workmanlike roll of tools, the mere possession of which rendered him liable to ten years' penal servitude. I shuddered as we found a cab and climbed into it.

And now I come to what is perhaps the most curious aspect of this tale. We had intended to leave the cab a few streets away from Jameson's shop, and do the last stretch on foot, just in case. Now, my friends will tell you that I am a down-to-earth man; I do not believe in ghosts, or Spiritualism, or automatic writing, or anything of that kind, nor can I lay claim to a Scots grandmother with 'the second sight.' And yet, as we neared the point at which we would leave the cab, and Raffles raised his stick to let the cabbie know that he wished to stop, I knew that something was wrong. Make no mistake, this was no fancy born of a guilty conscience. I have felt guilty, and apprehensive, often enough on these expeditions with Raffles to know that particular sensation! This was different. I have said I knew that something was amiss, and that is literally true. I knew with a certainty of knowledge that brooked no equivocation. And so, as Raffles raised his stick and prepared to speak to the cabbie, I gripped his wrist.

He stared at me.

'Don't stop, Raffles!' I whispered. 'Something's wrong!'

There was evidently something in my face which convinced him. 'What? What's wrong?'

'I don't know, but I know something is!'

He did tap the roof then, and told the

cabbie to drive down the road on which Jameson's shop front stood. As we rattled down the road I looked out of the window, and saw a figure lurking in a doorway, a few doors down from Jameson's shop. Raffles leaned over to me. 'Anyone your side?' he asked in a low tone.

'One.'

'And two this. Policemen, or I'm a monkey's uncle!' He tapped the roof again, and this time told the cabbie to take us along the lane which ran behind the shop.

There were more watchers there. I counted two, three, and then I gripped Raffles' arm again. 'Mackenzie!' I hissed. I need hardly remind you that Inspector Mackenzie of Scotland Yard was our old adversary. This was before he had put the handcuffs on me, or driven Raffles into hiding, but we knew he suspected us, and was only awaiting his chance.

The cab came to the end of the lane, and slowed. 'Straight on, cabbie!' said Raffles. We went on for a couple of streets, then Raffles added, 'My friend and I seem to have mistaken the address, cabbie. Would you wait here a moment?'

The man pulled the cab up, and Raffles and I got down, lit cigarettes, and wandered a few paces out of earshot to discuss strategies.

'I take it they are waiting for us?' I asked stupidly.

'Impossible that they are there for any other purpose, Bunny!'

'But how — I mean, why? Or do I mean 'how', after all?'

'As I read it,' said Raffles thoughtfully, 'Stourton has betrayed us to Mackenzie. Or to the Yard, at any rate.'

'But why? We were trying to help him, Raffles!'

'Ah, but he could not be sure of that. It was a fantastic affair, you must allow, Bunny, two complete strangers offering to help him replace stolen money? He thought about it in the cold light of day, and he got cold feet. He thought something would go wrong, that we should be caught and incriminate him. Or perhaps he decided that he did not dare trust us after all, concluded that we would merely make off with the cash. Suppose that were so, then when Jameson discovered his loss he would think at once of Stourton, whom Jameson already suspects, and with the money gone Stourton could not even hope to offer to give it back in exchange for clemency, as you suggested at one point. He could hardly tell the truth, for it is too fantastic for belief! What can he do?'

'What, Raffles?'

'Exactly what he did do! He thinks it over, and sends a note — anonymous, of course — to the Yard, saying that there will be an attempt on Jameson's shop, tonight or tomorrow night. Now, Stourton is safe whatever happens! If we are seen entering the shop, Mackenzie and his merry men move in and take us; it matters not whether the safe is open, or the cash is found on us, for Mackenzie has long had his suspicions of me, as you know. Let him find us where we should not be, on private premises at night, and that will suffice for him.'

I could see that, but I was still puzzled. 'And if we had run off with the cash and made no attempt to replace it?'

'Ah, in that event, once Jameson discovers the loss, Mackenzie would think that the theft had taken place last night, Saturday! Or that he and his men had somehow missed the thieves as they entered and left. I would not have put it past Mackenzie to search our rooms, and if the cash had been found there — well! In any case, Mackenzie has the anonymous note predicting the theft! Stourton is thus in the clear, whatever we did or did not do.'

'The little rat!'

'Yes, but it was an ingenious solution, Bunny. He neatly disposes of any lingering suspicion that Jameson may have of him. That was simple enough, but what I don't, and won't, understand, Bunny, is how you came to know that something was wrong?'

'Oh, my Aberdonian grandmother, Raffles. The second sight, and all that, you know. But what of the cash? As you say, when Jameson finds the tally falls short, Mackenzie may search our rooms anyway. I wouldn't put it past Stourton to have included our descriptions in his note!'

'Yes, indeed. 'A handsome young man about town, with an older, ill-favoured accomplice of dissipated and unpolished appearance', perhaps? Quite unmistakable, Bunny!'

'Raffles!'

'Yes, I believe you could be right. It is certainly odd that Mackenzie, of all the Scotland Yard men, should be lying in wait. It may be coincidence, of course, but then it may not. Anyway, Bunny, I don't see why this treacherous little eel should be allowed to wriggle off the hook.'

'I'm not sure that one uses a hook for eels, Raffles.'

'Well, then, I don't see why he should wriggle off whatever it is you do damned well catch eels with! Come along, we have work to do. Cabbie,' he added, strolling back to our driver, 'we have remembered the address,' and he mentioned a street no great distance from Stourton's house.

We covered the remaining distance on foot, and Raffles opened a side window without difficulty. We made our way to the room in which we had first heard

Stourton speak of his purloining his employer's money, and concealed the hatbox in a deliberately clumsy fashion.

'Now,' said Raffles as we made our way out once again, 'I'd like to watch the fun, if at all possible, Bunny. We need a place of concealment.' And he looked about him carefully, like any respectable citizen getting his bearings in strange surroundings.

'There's an empty house across the road,' I ventured, waving at the 'To Let' sign.

'Excellent, Bunny! We'll see the agents first thing tomorrow morning.' He glanced at his watch. 'Or later this morning, if we are to be pedantic.'

'And suppose nothing happens tomorrow — later today, I mean?'

'H'mm. In that event, we'll have to think of something else. But I imagine Mackenzie will be a little disenchanted by his fruitless vigil, and will want to make further enquiries.'

'Hang on — you said that Stourton's note to Mackenzie would be anonymous?'

'So it would. A perfectly sensible

precaution. But Mackenzie will know that Stourton is an employee of Jameson's. And besides, two can write anonymous notes!'

With that, I had to be satisfied. We returned to our separate abodes, and I slept like a log until Raffles banged on the door at some ungodly hour. It took me a moment to recollect what I was supposed to do, then I was up and dressed in a very short while. We collected the keys to my empty house from the agents, Raffles explaining that we preferred to look round unescorted, and saying that we did not know exactly when we should find time to inspect the house, so the agents were not to get worried if we did not return at once. The house was in an unfashionable area, and was unfurnished, so the agents made no objection to that, especially since Raffles slipped a couple of gold coins over the desk.

We went at once to the house, and made ourselves relatively comfortable upon the sill of a a large window which commanded a reasonable view of Stourton's house. This was silent, though the blinds were up. 'Gone to his work, I suppose,' said Raffles. 'But I'll wager he's back before long, and Mackenzie with him!'

I did not take the wager, which was as well, for at half past nine a cab rolled up to Stourton's house, and Mackenzie, Stourton, and a constable got down. Of course, we never found out just what had happened, though Raffles and I thought — and still think — that Mackenzie had indeed alerted Jameson to the anonymous letter, and asked the pawnbroker to check his safe. But perhaps Jameson had decided to anticipate slightly, and checked the safe independently? In any event, they had found cash missing, a lot of cash. Only a fool would neglect Stourton, an obvious suspect; and say what you would of Mackenzie, he was nobody's fool.

Stourton, naturally, had a jaunty air about him. He knew he had naught to fear, for the two strangers had the hatbox and its valuable contents! He did not exactly offer Mackenzie a cigar as they strode to the front door, but you could tell they were getting on famously.

Ten minutes passed, not more, before they came out into the street. But now Stourton was a changed man. I heard his voice, a plaintive wail, from across in my hiding place: 'But I don't know how it got there!' (True enough, thought I!) 'It shouldn't have been there!'

'You have the right of it, my lad,' said Mackenzie. 'It certainly should NOT have been there!' And off they went, the constable, Mackenzie, and the woeful Stourton.

I turned to Raffles, who was laughing away to himself. 'Got him, Bunny! Ah, well,' he added, as we let ourselves out and started back to the house agents, 'I had hoped for an easier task. But needs must. And the sight of that wretch's face was almost worth the three thousand!'

'Raffles?'

For answer, he took his hand out of his pocket, and showed me a slip of wax concealed within the palm. I recognized this as the sort of thing he had so often used to take an impression of a key or lock. 'Raffles?' I said again.

He sighed at my obtuseness. 'Bunny,

Bunny! Do I look like a philanthropist? I had intended to replace the missing cash last night. That would have got Stourton off that hook of which we spoke, but it would also have put the pawnbroker in a good mood, a relaxed mood, an expensive mood, a love-thy-neighbour mood. Above all things, Bunny, an unsuspicious mood! I expected the job of opening the safe to take some little time, but I planned to take a wax impression, and then make my own key at my leisure, so that it would take mere moments to open the safe a second time.'

'Oh! And clear out the entire contents?'

Raffles nodded, then sighed. 'It means the hard work is still to do, but I'd have had to do it last night anyway, so I'll think of it as labour deferred. But I do begrudge that three thousand in the hatbox, Bunny! For I suspect that Mackenzie will retain that as evidence. Still, he may not; the case against Stourton is clearly proved, the cash may be back in the safe even now. You'd better get two hatboxes, Bunny, not just one. Stout ones, mind, gold is heavy.'

'Really?' I asked with what sarcasm I could manage, but it was wasted.

In the event, though the safe was well stocked, one hatbox proved sufficient. And I rather fancy you can guess who had to lug the confounded thing over half London?

5

THE MAHARAJAH'S JEWELS

'The start of a new season, Bunny,' said AJ Raffles. He spoke in an absent-minded fashion, and he did not look at me as he said the words, nor did he look out of the window at the sunshine of a beautiful morning in late April. Instead his gaze was fixed upon the great wooden chest which had given me some dreadful days during the previous year when Raffles, all unbeknownst to me, had hidden in the wretched thing in order to rob a bank vault.

Since his re-emergence from the secret sliding panel in the lid of the chest, rather in the manner of some saucy wood nymph, or whatever more appropriate creature of Greek myth the classically learned reader may choose to imagine, the chest had stood in a corner of his rooms in the Albany, filled with the proceeds of our various villainies. He lit a Sullivan, and turned to face me, raising an eyebrow as if to ask a question.

'If you're thinking what I think you're thinking — ' I began.

'Try not to sound like a third-rate music hall comedy turn! And above all, be reasonable, Bunny!'

'Reasonable!'

'If you had any notion of the work that went into that chest, you wouldn't quibble like this. Weeks it took to get it right! And I had to do it all myself, for of course I could never trust any workman with the job. It's a crying shame to have it stand there useless, when it might be earning its keep.'

'It is earning its keep,' I said shortly. 'It's full of silver, which is, when all is said and done, its primary function.'

'Ah, and there's another thing,' said Raffles earnestly. 'It's high time I emptied the thing, and sold off the bits and pieces of plate which are in there. Too dangerous by half, my boy! Especially with Mackenzie nosing round,' he added thoughtfully.

'Oh, Mackenzie's nosing around, is he?'

I asked with all the scorn I could manage. Raffles said nothing, but his eyebrow lifted again. I was not to be fooled quite that easily, though! You may perhaps recall that on the last occasion that Raffles used the chest, he pretended that Inspector Mackenzie of Scotland Yard, our old adversary, had been suspicious of us, and that he — Raffles, I mean — wanted to clear some stolen silver out of his rooms for safety. The idea was, said Raffles, that the chest, complete with the plunder, would be lodged at my bank, in the vault. Meantime, Raffles himself would quit London, and thereby leave the field clear for Mackenzie to search the rooms and prove them blameless. A less complicated scheme than many which Raffles had proposed to me, and a convincing tale. I was taken in. In all innocence I took the obnoxious container to my bank.

I then heard that the bank vault had been robbed, and you may imagine my sentiments when I realized that the police would be all over the place, and that they might open the chest to see if it had been rifled! A second thought was that the chest might already have been opened by the criminals and the stolen goods laid bare to the public gaze! The hours subsequent to these reflections are best left unmentioned.

Of course — as anyone but myself must have known from the very outset — it was Raffles himself, hidden in the chest, who had committed the robbery. Well, as I say, there would not be a second time; and I set my features into what I fervently hoped was a cynical sneer.

'Oh, Mackenzie really is suspicious, I assure you,' said Raffles. He went over to the chest, and threw the lid back. 'In fact, I've made a start, as you may see.'

Much against my better judgement, for I had resolved, as I say, to have naught to do with his madcap scheme, I cast a glance at the interior of the chest, and was surprised to see that it held nothing but a couple of small dishes, little bigger than ashtrays, and a delicate silver cup and stand, some four inches high. 'And the cup's my own,' Raffles complained. 'First one I was ever given for my cricket, back at school.' And he took it from the chest, and stood it on the mantel shelf, then placed the two dishes on the little table by the window. 'Safe enough, I fancy, they are ordinary enough not to be positively identified.' He tapped the chest significantly. 'All ready for action, Bunny.'

Doubt began to creep upon me. 'So Mackenzie really and truly is sniffing round, this time?'

Raffles nodded. ''Fraid so, Bunny. Which means that the whole scheme is dashed dangerous.'

'As far as I'm concerned, it means that the dashed scheme is damned from the start,' I told him plainly.

He said nothing, but took a copy of one of the popular weekly papers from the table, and threw it across to me. It was folded open at the society 'gossip' page, and I saw the usual nonsense about who was expected to arrive in London for the season, and when, and where they would be staying. 'Read it,' Raffles told me.

'Oh, very well! 'Arriving next week is a glittering array — ' really, Raffles!'

'Carry on. Just the names, if you wish.'

'Names, then. 'The alert observer may hope to espy the Duke and Duchess of -- - -; the bearded and rugged features of Sir Paul Chapman, the African explorer and gold magnate' — drivel, Raffles! — 'the American tobacco magnate Mr John T Hardiman III and Mrs Hardiman; the Hon. Matthew Booth, younger son of the Earl of - - - -' — I know him, Raffles, the silly young ass! — 'the Maharajah of Cummerbund — ''

'Stop there.'

'What, the Maharajah of Cummerbund?' I put the paper down. 'I don't believe there is such a place!'

'Oh, there is,' said Raffles. 'What d'you think the article of natty gent's evening apparel is named after, then? Famous hill station. Very famous club there, too, the Cummerbund Club. In fact, with your aspirations to social climbing, I'm surprised — '

'And even if there is any such place, I've certainly never heard of a Maharajah of it.'

'There's a photograph of him on another page,' said Raffles, waving a hand at the paper. ' 'Fabulously wealthy' is, I believe, the correct, if hackneyed, phrase. I played for IZ against him back in '81. Of course he was only the Rajah, then. And younger too — 'eheu, fugaces!' And about twenty stones lighter.'

'A lot of fellows go to seed a bit as they get on. Matter of fact, I myself have noticed — '

'Oh, there's a reason for the corpulence, Bunny. His Royal Fabulousness has himself weighed against jewels on every birthday.'

'What, and then gives them away to the deserving poor?'

'Bunny, Bunny! No, if he tips the scale, which he invariably does, then his tax-gatherers go out and make up the difference by grinding the faces of his people. Yes, he always was a rotter, even as Rajah. And no great shakes as a cricketer, come to that, would never have made the team had his father not owned it. It would be a positive benefaction to relieve him of some of his ill-gotten gains. A work of charity, my boy.'

'Well, charity begins at home, so you

can count me out.'

He shook his head sadly. 'For a literary man, your phraseology leaves much to be desired, Bunny.'

'Perhaps it does — hang on, though, is this fellow weighed against the jewels here, or back home?'

'Back home, of course. The Savoy, grand though it may be, has no facilities for that sort of thing.'

'Well then, since I take it you have your eye on these jewels, and since I further take it that we are not travelling to India, he must bring the jewels over here, yes?' Raffles smiled and nodded. 'Now, why does he do that?' I asked suspiciously.

'Fear,' said Raffles shortly. 'He's terrified that he might be slung out in absentia, and thinks that if he leaves the jewels there they might be seized if his people do rise up against him.'

'H'mm. That makes sense.' (From which you will deduce that Raffles' persuasive powers were already beginning to set at naught my better judgement!)

He went on: 'As it is, this would be the one and only opportunity for the determined thief, for he has an entourage of guards as villainous as himself, armed to the teeth.'

'Eunuchs?'

'Very likely,' said Raffles. 'Not that it's the sort of thing a chap likes to ask about. But it would be typical of the man. And since deficiency in one department is often compensated for by over-development in another, they're as strong as horses — geldings, then — and ill-tempered to boot.'

I shook my head. 'Be that as it may, if you insist upon doing this stupid thing, you do it alone.'

'So be it, Bunny. I won't go on about never thinking you were one to let a fellow down, or anything of that sort, but I confess I'd sooner have had you in it with me.'

'Consider the risk!' I said with all the fervour of which I was capable. 'If Mackenzie is, as you say, suspicious, then he will surely be paying special attention to you, and to me, and to these rooms.'

'And yet the trick worked once,' said Raffles, a far-away note in his voice. 'Even you never suspected!'

'But don't you see that it was because I never suspected that the trick worked, Raffles? You yourself have said that my innocent face is worth — oh, I don't know — a whole regiment of cracksmen!'

He laughed at this. 'Perhaps I don't esteem you quite that high, Bunny, but I take your point. Your face is indeed my fortune, or it has been more than once, and I've said so more than once. But don't you, in your turn, see that now you are in on the trick, it would be that much easier? You take the chest to your bank — '

'And there's another thing. How on earth can you know that this Maharajah will deposit his worldly goods in any bank, let alone mine?'

'He always does,' said Raffles, very seriously. 'Each season he sends his jewels and what have you over in advance, lodges them at the bank — your bank, my Bunny, the City and Suburban, Sloane Street branch — to be called for. The dibs are there a good week before he turns up to collect them. I'm rather surprised you didn't know, I'd have thought the clerks would have boasted about it. Must be very discreet, your bankers. His wife's picture is in there, too. Rather fine woman, don't you think?'

'He only has the one, then?' I sneered. 'I should have thought it wouldn't be worth stealing just one Maharani's jewels.'

'No,' he answered, with not the slightest trace of anger at my words, 'the one is, I assure you, quite sufficient. Remarkable woman. But not a serious proposition from a burglar's viewpoint, for I know the lady carries her own jewels about her person, never lets them out of her sight, which is very wise, given her husband's criminal tendencies. No, Bunny, it's the gentleman's own sparklers that attract me. And, as I keep telling you, the trick worked once and there's no reason why it wouldn't, and shouldn't, work again. The crook hides in the chest, which you take — his accomplice, that is to say, takes — to the bank. The Maharajah's goods are already in there, so the crook waits for nightfall, makes his selection, and leaves a bit of a mess, breaks open the door, or what have you, just like last time. The very next day the bank officials discover the theft, assume the crook has left with the takings, call the police, and there's the devil of a fuss. What more natural than that you — the accomplice, I mean — and the other customers, should want to recover their goods, to make sure they're safe? It worked last time, and it'll work this. All you have to do, Bunny — '

'Raffles!'

'Very well, then, all you would have had to do is take the chest to your bank, wait for tomorrow and the fuss — '

'Tomorrow?'

'Oh, yes. I am somewhat better informed than the writer of that society column. The Maharajah's wealth is safe and secure even now, now, very now, my Bunny. So, tomorrow there would have been a fuss, and you would recover the chest! What could be — could have been, I mean to say — more straightforward or simple?' And he lit another Sullivan.

'Raffles!' I looked out of the window, my heart full of sorrow, anger and bitterness in equal parts. He never spoke, and I stood there, miserable and silent, for a long moment. Then: 'Raffles?'

'Well?'

'Raffles, are you really determined to go through with this?'

'Absolutely and irrevocably, Bunny. If you won't help me, there's an end of it, I'll send for the doorman and spin him some yarn or another.'

'And expect him to recover the chest in case of alarm, I suppose?' I said sardonically, or as sardonically as I could manage.

He shrugged.

'It's a two-man job, Raffles, and well you know it! Very well, then — if I must, I must.'

He clapped his hands, and smiled broadly. 'I knew I could rely on you, Bunny! Now, go down and get the man to send for a cab, and then bring him back up here, for it's also a two-man job moving the chest, as you know.'

'To my cost! But what of the necessities?'

For answer, he held up a silver hip flask and a paper packet of what I took to be sandwiches. 'I dare not take cigarettes,' he

173

said quite seriously, 'for the aroma might give me away. But this will do for the one night, I fancy. Now lock me in, and keep the key, purely in case of emergency, and then be off with you, Bunny, and fetch the doorman up here!'

He stepped into the chest, and lowered the lid carefully. I did as he had told me, locked the lid and pocketed the key, and then sought out the doorman, and brought him back to Raffles' rooms. The man looked round. 'Mr Raffles gone out?' he asked, not in any way suspicious, but merely making conversation. 'He did say he might be away for a day or two.'

'Yes, that's right,' I said. 'He wants the chest lodged safe at the bank during his absence.'

The man shook his head and clicked his tongue, obviously chagrined that Raffles should so mistrust the alertness of the staff of the Albany, and the doorman in particular, but he made no remark as we toiled down the stairs with the chest — which was of a solid, not to say weighty, construction.

Now, I have told you all the thoughts

174

and misgivings that had gone through my mind, so you will readily believe that I was in what might reasonably be described as a somewhat nervy condition as I stood beside the chest waiting for the cab which the doorman had summoned. I could not swear to it, to this day, but as I glanced about me and took out a cigarette, on the opposite side of the road I fancied I saw the lean and angular form of Inspector Mackenzie! I looked away hastily, lest he catch my eye and come over, and when I ventured to glance back the road was empty.

It might be pure nerves, sheer imagination, I told myself. Might be? It must be. Still, had the doorman not been waiting patiently less than six feet away, I think I would have made some remark, for I knew that Raffles would have heard perfectly well a warning spoken within a few feet of the chest; the holes he had cut in it to permit observation and breathing also allowed him to hear tolerably well. But the man stood there like a rock, so I dare not speak. The best I could do was tap gently on the lid of the chest, and hope that Raffles had seen Mackenzie, if indeed Mackenzie it had been. I was considerably heartened when my tap was answered by the gentlest of knocks from within the chest.

Still, heartened or no, I could have kicked myself. So Raffles had been telling the truth — for once! To be frank with you, reader, I had suspected that all that nonsense about Mackenzie had been just that, nonsense told by Raffles to impress me with his crackpot scheme. And I had gone along with it, half fearful, yet half laughing to myself at the secret knowledge that Raffles was exaggerating, that there was danger, to be sure, but no more danger than the usual. But if Raffles had not been spinning me a yarn? If Mackenzie were taking an interest in us, if Mackenzie had been lurking outside the Albany — and I dared not finish the thought, it was too horrible to contemplate.

The fact that I had tapped upon the chest and Raffles had answered, I was now inclined to discount. It might all too easily have been that he thought I was reassuring him that all was well, and that he was acknowledging what he imagined was a message of support and solace! If that were so, if Raffles had not seen Mackenzie, had not realized the true import of my impromptu message —

Before I could attempt to formulate some strategy to take account of my changed frame of mind, the cab drew up, and the doorman bawled out the address of my bank to the driver! And then, before I could speak — not that I had the least notion of what I might have said — the doorman and the cabbie had lifted the chest on to the roof of the cab, and the doorman was holding the cab door open for me. In my agitation I entirely forgot to tip him, and his reproachful, 'Thank YOU, sir!' as the cab pulled away was about the single redeeming feature of the whole sorry business.

As the cab rattled along Piccadilly I slumped back in my seat and thought furiously. What on earth was I to do? Damn Raffles and all his rotten schemes, for they invariably caused me more grief and heartache than the proceeds warranted! My anger at Raffles grew as I sat there, until it ousted all thoughts of anything else, so that it was not until the cab actually drew up outside my bank, and the doorman stepped forward, that I realized what I ought to have done. I ought, of course, to have told the cabbie to take me to my own rooms in Mount Street! It was obvious, now I realized it! Home; my own fireside. Once there, I could have moved the chest, and Raffles, to safety, and explained the whole situation to him at leisure. As it was, it was still not too late, though, and as the cabbie and the bank doorman between them made a start on lifting the chest down from the roof, I bleated, 'I say! I should have said 'Mount Street', not — ' and I broke off, for advancing towards us from the bank doorway was — of all men — Inspector Mackenzie!

The cabbie and the doorman had placed the chest on the ground, and were looking at me with that curious expression of men who feel they have just wasted valuable time and energy at the behest of a fool. Mackenzie stopped in front of me, and regarded me with a cynical eye. 'A fine day, Mr Manders.'

'It is indeed — Inspector Mackenzie.'

'You'll be leaving your chest for safe-keeping, I take it?'

'Oh, absolutely, Inspector Mackenzie,' I said, as loudly as I dared.

'It's surprising the number of people who are doing the same just now. I suspect it's a consequence of the press reports that the Maharajah of Cummerbund patronizes this branch of the bank.'

'Is that so, Inspector Mackenzie?' He stepped back involuntarily at the blast of sound I produced. 'I haven't seen any of those reports, Inspector Mackenzie.' How I hoped that Raffles would hear me, and modify his plans accordingly!

'No? Well, that's what I think would account for the large numbers of folk leaving chests and the like. You may be sure we'll take care — good care — of your possessions, Mr Manders, for we've been asked special to keep an eye on the Maharajah's goods, and yours will be in there with them.'

'Is that so, Inspector Mackenzie? It's very reassuring to know that the POLICE are paying the bank such particular attention, INSPECTOR Mackenzie.' To the waiting men, I said, or croaked, rather, for my voice was going with the effort of trying to make Raffles hear me, 'That's right. The chest is to go down to the vault. If Inspector MACKENZIE would just be so kind as to step to one side?'

I fancied I heard a muttered remark or two from cabbie and doorman as to the advisability of making up one's blinking mind, but they took the chest into the bank, leaving me standing there perspiring more freely than the spring weather could account for.

Mackenzie looked at me, then his gaze wandered down the street. 'Your friend Mr Raffles isn't with you?' he asked casually.

'Raffles? Raffles? Oh, no, he's — that is, I understand he's out of town at the moment.'

'Indeed? I'd have thought he'd be watching the cricket or something of the kind, him being so fond of the game.'

'Cricket? Is there any cricket? No, no, I fancy he's out of town. Couldn't say for certain, though, I haven't seen him for a day or two.' I babbled away all unthinking, and regretted the lie as soon as it was told, for if it were Mackenzie I had spotted at the Albany, then he would know that I had been at Raffles' rooms not an hour before! But he made no reply, merely nodding thoughtfully, then he raised his hat and strolled casually into the bank.

My emotions are perhaps better imagined than described. Surely Raffles must have heard me, for I had bawled out 'Inspector Mackenzie' a dozen times at least, at the top of my voice! Raffles would hear, he would understand, he would make no move, commit no robbery as planned, but remain safe within the chest until I collected it, and him.

With that thought, which should have brought me some ease from the turmoil of mind I was in, came a new horror. With Mackenzie lurking round the bank premises, how could I possibly collect the chest immediately after I had left it? I would have to wait, do nothing for a respectable interval, or it would look idiotic, and not merely idiotic but downright suspicious as well! Raffles had his flask, true, and his paper of sandwiches, but that would scarcely suffice for more than a day, two at best.

I took the cab back to my own rooms, poured myself the largest and strongest whisky and soda for many a long year, and sat down to think the matter over. After half an hour I came to the conclusion that there was only one sensible thing to do. The very next morning I would go round to the bank, and tell them that I needed the silver — no, that wouldn't do! Very well, I would tell them that I had forgotten to put some other pieces in the chest, and must take it away with me. True, that would add to the reputation for idiosyncrasy, if not downright eccentricity, which my financial dealings at the bank had already earned me, but what of that? The main, the essential, the only thing was that Raffles must be rescued at all costs.

My mind made up to that, I set off for my club, to stop, horror-stricken, at my door. Suppose that Raffles had not heard all my bellows of 'Inspector Mackenzie' and the rest? Suppose that he had not seen the inspector outside the Albany? Suppose that I arrived at the bank to find alarums and excursions, the police in possession, Raffles taken, myself sought as an accomplice?

I told myself a dozen, a hundred, a thousand times that I was being foolish. But I could not face the club, and I found that I could not bring myself to sleep, or even to rest, such was my agitation of mind. I sat up in an armchair for the whole of that wretched night, falling asleep at last in the small hours of the morning, and waking with the dawn with a stiff neck and a most appalling headache.

I had no mind for breakfast, but found that I could manage a cup of strong coffee. I will confess that I toyed with the notion of something stronger yet, but dismissed it quickly, for if I were to extricate Raffles from this shambles of his own devising I would need a clear head; moreover, if Mackenzie were to put the darbies about my wrists, it would be for burglary alone, and not for being drunk and incapable to boot!

* ★ ★

I fretted as the hours dragged by until the business world would start work, and as soon as I decently could I summoned a cab and drove round to the bank. It seemed to me that I could spot one or two men of the detective persuasion hanging about the premises, but I told myself I was being overly mistrustful.

The clerk — the same one who had supervised the depositing of the chest the day before — regarded me with a sardonic eye as I stammered out my tale of having forgotten to put some pieces in the chest, but he had his men bring the vile thing from the lower depths, and load it on to the cab. I was about to climb in myself, when I felt a light touch upon my elbow.

I looked round, and almost fainted

when I saw that it was none other than Mackenzie! At his side was a tall, slim Indian gentleman, in a beautifully tailored suit.

Mackenzie turned to his companion and said, 'Your Highness, I don't believe you know Mr Manders? Mr Manders, His Highness the Maharajah of Cummerbund.'

'Aah — ' I could not tell you just what I tried to stammer out, but the Maharajah shook my hand, a firm manly grip, then told me, 'You must excuse me, Mr Manders. We appear to have a small emergency.' And he nodded at Mackenzie, and strode off into the bank.

'Was that really the Maharajah of Cummerbund?' I whispered.

Mackenzie nodded. 'A pity Mr Raffles isn't here, for he knows His Highness well. His Highness tells me the two of them used to play many practical jokes on each other. And I happen to know that the Maharajah holds the distinction of being the only man ever to score six sixes in one over off Mr Raffles' bowling. Or so they tell me; I don't follow the cricket myself.' He looked curiously at me. 'Are you quite well, Mr Manders?'

'Oh, yes, yes!' But I lied; for the man whose hand I had just shaken — tall, slim, handsome, athletic — was a far cry from the image which Raffles had planted in my mind! I had not, of course, looked for the photograph of the Maharajah which the serpent Raffles had claimed was in the newspaper; I had taken Raffles' word for it. I simply could not understand why Raffles should have lied to me. One of those practical jokes Mackenzie had mentioned, perhaps?

I could not tell you what else I may or may not have thought, or said; in any event Mackenzie brushed my feeble whimperings aside. 'Taking your chest away so soon, Mr Manders?' said he.

'Yes, yes, I — that is, I quite forgot to put some bits and pieces in there — '

'I'm afraid I shall have to ask you to open the chest, Mr Manders.'

My heart all but stopped. I managed, 'Open it? But why?'

Mackenzie looked round, and lowered his voice. 'The fact is, sir, we have information that some enterprising crimi-nal plans a robbery, here, at the bank. That's why the Maharajah's here, he keeps his own bits and pieces at this branch, as you know.'

'Information? 'Plans', you say?'

'We have our sources, Mr Manders.'

'But this — this robbery — this planned robbery — it hasn't taken place yet, has it? That is — '

'Well, sir,' said Mackenzie, a grim glint in his eye, 'that's what we're trying to find out. Now, it's true that there is no sign of forced entry — '

'Ah, well! There you are, then!' said I, recovering my scattered wits slightly.

'But we're by no means sure that the thief hasn't opened some of the chests and boxes and what have you, removed some of the contents, and locked up again after him.'

'Surely — '

'So,' Mackenzie continued inexorably, 'we're asking all those who take their boxes and so on away if they'll be so kind as to co-operate with us and take a quick look, just to be sure. After all, Mr

Manders, you wouldn't want to find your valuables missing when you do open your chest, now would you?'

'Oh, no, absolutely not! So I'll be sure to check, first thing, once I get home, and let you know at once if — '

'If you'd be so kind as to take a quick look now, sir. I'll just stand here, and you can tell me if anything's gone.'

'Look here — '

'Of course, if there's some good reason why you'd rather not — ' and Mackenzie left the rest unspoken.

'Oh, no! Rather not!' I stared at him unhappily, and then at the chest.

Mackenzie stood there for a long moment, then he cleared his throat delictely. 'You'll have the key there, sir?'

'Oh, yes. Rather.' I stared at him again. 'Look here, Inspector — '

'Sir?'

I squared my shoulders.

This was it, was it? The end of the road?

Well, we had had a good innings, Raffles and I, but we had always known that one day the wicket must fall to

Mackenzie, or someone like him. I had wished it might be otherwise, but now that our doom was upon us, I would play my part as best I could. 'I really don't think it's at all appropriate to open the thing here, in the street, do you, Inspector?'

He nodded, understanding. 'Perhaps not, sir. Shall I have it taken into the bank again, where we can be a touch more private, as it were?'

I nodded dumbly. Mackenzie waved to a couple of the men whom I had earlier suspected of being policemen, and they silently carried the chest into the bank, past the astonished clerks, and into the assistant manager's office. The assistant manager had evidently been alerted to the fact that something was in the wind, for he shot me a venomous look and then made himself scarce, leaving Mackenzie, a couple of plain-clothes policemen, and myself.

'Mr Manders?' Mackenzie nodded at the chest.

Reluctantly, I took the key from my pocket. 'The lock hasn't been opened, or tampered with, or anything, you see,' I said, in a last desperate attempt to salvage something.

'If you would, sir.'

I put the key in the lock, turned it, and took hold of the lid. Before I could open the chest, Mackenzie held up a hand. 'Mr Manders, I must ask you formally if this chest is your property.'

'What? Yes, of course it is.'

'Only you were seen bringing it from Mr Raffles' apartment in the Albany.' So he had been there, thought I! 'That being the case,' he went on, 'I just wanted to be quite sure that it is yours, and that you were, and are, not simply acting for Mr Raffles.'

For a moment, I hesitated. I could say that the chest was not my property, but that of Raffles, and that I was merely acting on his instructions when I took it to and from the bank.

That would not help Raffles himself, it is true, but then he was lost anyway, once Mackenzie opened the chest. By denying Raffles, I might help him, I could stay at liberty and — somehow — work to free him.

As I say, I hesitated, but I can say with honesty that it was only for a moment. Then, with what dignity I could muster, I squared my shoulders a second time, and told Mackenzie, 'The chest itself is Mr Raffles' property, but he let me borrow it. I take full responsibility for the contents.' I have always thought that Iscariot was virtuous in the extreme compared with the other chap — whose name escapes me — who twice — or was it thrice — betrayed a man he had called a friend.

'Very well,' said Mackenzie, and threw open the lid.

I was looking at Mackenzie, not at the chest, and I saw his face change. But it was not a change which indicated that my worst fears were justified; on the contrary, it was sheer astonishment.

Following his gaze, I glanced into the chest, to see — three dented and tarnished salvers in EPNS, and bad EPNS at that, one pewter beer mug with a dubiously 'comic' inscription and illustration engraved upon it, and a German silver candelabrum of the most hideous design it has been my misfortune to encounter. Total value, perhaps three shillings and sixpence, was my estimate.

For a long time, Mackenzie stared in silence at this egregious display of bad taste. Then he swallowed with some difficulty, and said, 'Is this really what you deposited in the bank vault?'

'Certainly!' I told him airily. 'It may not be much, but it's all mine, honestly acquired. And, if you were wondering, nothing has been stolen.'

'Stolen?' he said quickly.

'You recall that you wanted me to open the chest lest any property of mine had been stolen,' I reminded him gently.

'Ah, to be sure.' He flushed, but then recovered his composure somewhat. He lifted the candelabrum cautiously, and stared at it. 'Alloy, Mr Manders?'

'Well, we can't all afford the real thing, Inspector. Immense sentimental value, you know.'

'And you say you omitted to deposit more of the same?'

'Absolutely. Stacks of it. Easy overlooked. I'm sure you know how it is? Anyway, if there's nothing more — ' And

I left him standing there, swept regally past the assistant manager — ignoring the craven dog's halting offers of assistance — and in a lordly fashion I called the bank's messenger to take the chest outside, and be damned quick about it.

The cab was still there, the cabbie sitting with a look half bemused and half amused, and the messengers loaded the chest on to the roof. I was about to climb into the cab when my ingress was halted a second time by a touch on the arm, and a familiar voice.

'Bunny! What are you doing, old chap?'

'Raffles? Raffles!'

That was all I could manage. I think I may flatter myself that I had recovered my composure in an exemplary fashion under Mackenzie's gaze a moment before, but by this time I did not even have sufficient wit left to stammer out my tale about taking the chest home.

'Ah, Mr Raffles.' It was Mackenzie, who had followed me out of the bank, and stood staring at Raffles with a curious expression. 'We hadn't seen you for a while, and were wondering just what might have become of you.'

'Oh,' said Raffles vaguely, 'I've been out of town for a day or so. Heard my old pal the Maharajah of Cummerbund was here, so thought I'd come back and look him up. But what on earth is happening here? Bunny, where on earth are you going with that prestigious coffer?'

'Home, Raffles!' Of that, if of nothing else in the great wide world, I was certain. And I was equally certain that my first action would be to prepare for myself a brandy and soda that would dwarf all others of its ilk; a B&S that men would write poems — nay, positive sagas — about; a B&S that would be remembered in the annals of self-indulgence for several centuries.

And my second action? Why, to eliminate Raffles, of course, remove him from the face of the earth before he could devise any more idiotic schemes. I gripped his elbow firmly, lest he harbour thoughts of escaping my just and righteous vengeance. 'And you, Raffles — you are coming with me, Raffles.'

'If you insist, then by all means I shall

go with you, Bunny.' And he leapt into the cab, and gave the driver the address.

It took a while for me to recover my wits, and I tried to stammer out a question, but Raffles would have none of it, waving me to silence and handing me a Sullivan. 'Later, my Bunny,' he said. 'Later.'

We arrived at Mount Street, and somehow or other got that damnable chest upstairs and into a corner. I poured myself that brandy and soda, and drank deep thereof. 'And now,' I began.

'One of the best schemes yet, I fancy, Bunny,' said Raffles, lighting a Sullivan.

'But how did you get out of the chest? When?'

'Through the secret door, of course, even you must have realized that. As for when, it was, naturally, when you left my rooms to fetch the doorman. I nipped into the bathroom, and there you are — or, there I was.'

'But you can't have been!' Raffles raised an eyebrow, and I hurried on, 'I tapped the lid of the chest out in the road, and you answered!'

'Not I, Bunny, I assure you. How could I, when I was upstairs in my rooms?'

'But I heard you!'

He shook his head, then smiled. 'I fancy it was the contents of the chest shifting that you heard, Bunny. Quite likely, given that you had just lugged the thing down the Albany stairs. A certain amount of settling was only to be expected.'

'Good Lord! Yes, you must be right. And I thought it was you! It was that which made me so anxious when Mackenzie — oh, but you couldn't know, could you? Mackenzie met me at the bank, mentioned the Maharajah, said the police had been tipped off — oh!'

Raffles nodded gently. 'And of course, when Mackenzie received the anonymous letter, he naturally thought of you and me. Most unworthy of him!' And he blew a smoke ring at the ceiling.

'And there's another thing — you lied to me about the Maharajah! You said he was a rotter, and surrounded by eunuchs, and — and — '

'How on earth did you ever gain that

impression from my murmurings, Bunny? You can't have been listening. Why, old Chandra is a marvellous chap, old friend of mine, brilliant cricketer, great philanthropist — '

'But what on earth was the point of it?' I asked, puzzled.

For answer, Raffles put a hand in his pocket, and pulled out a fistful of jewels; an emerald necklace and bracelets, sapphires, diamonds. 'Formerly the property of Mrs John T Hardiman III,' he said.

I put a hand to my head, then remembered. 'Wife of the American tobacco millionaire?'

'The very same. I needed a distraction, Bunny, for Mackenzie really is becoming dashed suspicious. But even he cannot guard two places at once, and since he was looking after the bank, the way was clear for me!' He glanced at the clock, and stood up. 'And I must be off, Bunny, for the lady herself should be getting up any time now — she is, I understand, a late riser — and she, or more likely her maid, will soon discover that all is not as it should be. It wouldn't do for Inspector

Mackenzie to find me here with these trinkets, so I'll away and dispose of them safely.'

'You think Mackenzie will suspect you?'

'Oh, he must, Bunny! I make fun of the fellow, but he's nobody's fool. He'll wipe the egg from his face, and do what he can. Let's just hope it isn't enough.' He paused at the door, and gazed at the chest. 'But it really was a shame not to work that trick properly. There really are some truly remarkable treasures in that bank vault, you know, Bunny. And I don't think that even Mackenzie would dare to enquire of you again, for no man enjoys being made to look foolish a second time. That being so, I suppose — '

By that time, though, I had recollected what my second action was to have been. I turned to the fireplace and picked up the poker. When I turned back, Raffles had gone, so I never did learn just what it was that he may, or may not, have supposed.

6

CHIEF MAZAWA

'Ever heard of Chief Mazawa, Bunny?' asked AJ Raffles.

'What, the — ?' I said, using a somewhat opprobrious term for men of colour, much in vogue at that time.

Raffles frowned. 'I have never cared very much for that word,' he told me. 'And in this instance it seems particularly inappropriate, for he can, according to the popular press, trace his ancestry back further than most of the Royal houses of Europe. And certainly further back than you or I.'

'In that event, I humbly beg the gentleman's pardon,' said I, and meant it. I regarded Raffles closely. 'But what is your interest in the fellow?'

Raffles' frown deepened. 'I'm not absolutely sure, Bunny, not at this early stage of the game. He's wealthy, of course, and that immediately piques my interest. But he intrigues me for other reasons, as well. However, you haven't answered the question which I really meant to put to you: what do you, an avid reader of the society gossip columns, know of him?'

'African, of course. Chief of some obscure tribe, the — ' I glanced at the weekly paper that lay upon the table close at hand — 'yes, the Ngoro tribe. Never heard of them, I must say.'

'No,' said Raffles slowly. 'And you are not alone in that, Bunny. I was talking to Professor Morton-Pyke, of the School of African Studies, and he was clearly no better informed than you are, or, for that matter, than I am. He hid it, of course, under a fog of speculation and abstruse but ambiguous terminology, as these academics do.'

'I've heard of some giant volcano called something like Ngorongoro,' I said. 'Wonder if that's named after the tribe?'

Raffles stared at me with some interest. 'H'mm. An intriguing thesis. Continue.'

'Tremendously wealthy, as you say,

though nobody knows the precise source of his wealth. All sorts of speculation as to that, of course. Over here to visit the Queen, so rumour has it. Don't quite know why, though. A bit of a mystery man all round, in fact. Made quite a hit with the public and the press, as you intimated.'

'Yes. The only public fact that seems incontrovertible is that of his wealth. I have it on good authority that when he first arrived in London, he was followed by a band of street urchins who called out the name of a popular and refreshing brand of tea — '

'Mazawatee!' I exclaimed.

'Exactly so. Anyway — '

'Wonder if the tea was named after him?'

Raffle smiled. 'Just as the volcano was named after the tribe of which he is the chief?'

It was my turn to stare at him. 'From your tone, I gather you are a trifle sceptical, Raffles?'

He shook his head quickly. 'Say, rather, that I begin to wonder if there are not too many coincidences associated with the chief. Anyway, as I was saying, these urchins were pestering him, and, as many people do, he threw a handful of coins for them to scramble for, to be rid of them. Only, my Bunny, he did not throw copper, nor yet silver! No, it was gold sovereigns he cast before these little ones!'

'Really?'

He nodded. 'Fact. A whole handful of them. I had it from a reliable source who was present, and who privately informed me that he — the reliable source, I mean — came precious close to abandoning his dignity and scrambling with the urchins!'

'I'd not have hesitated!' I said plainly, for to be blunt my finances were in a more than usually parlous state at the time — though when were they not?

Raffles laughed. 'I must confess that the weight of my own wallet would not test the weakest of men.'

'Hence your interest in Chief Mazawa?'

'You read my mind, Bunny.' He grew serious again. 'But I confess I'm puzzled by one aspect of his visit, one which you mentioned just now. Namely, why exactly is he here? I have heard some tales, mark you, tales that he is the chief of a large and remote area of land which is fabulously rich in minerals, gold, diamonds, even rubies. Now, mark that word, 'remote', Bunny. His lands are so remote that nobody knows quite where they are, some say near the borders of Tanganyika, some say north of Rhodesia, and so on. But in any event they are so remote that they have so far been free from traders and missionaries and any so-called 'civilizing influence', which is not necessarily a bad thing.'

'Amen to that!' I hesitated. 'Ah — but what has that to do with — ?'

'With us? The story I heard — or one of them, at any rate — is that he is here to come to some arrangement with one of the great mining houses, to sign a contract whereby they will exploit the mineral wealth of Mazawa's lands, paying him a proportion of the profits, and — and this is the crucial point, Bunny — ensuring that no other government or commercial interest makes inroads into his country. What d'you think to that?

Does it make sense?'

I thought it over for a moment. 'It could make a good deal of sense,' I said. 'Proper mining techniques would mean that even if old Mazawa were to receive merely a tenth part of what is produced it might well be far more than could be got by his tribesmen using primitive hand tools. Depending on the precise arrangements he makes, of course, he could easily get much more. And the political proposition is masterly, for one of the big mining enterprises will have armed guards and what have you to protect their interests, their own private army, almost, like old Rhodes, and will thereby ensure that only a very determined force could take the place over. By giving up a little, this Mazawa fellow is ensuring that the bulk will remain safe. He is clearly nobody's fool.'

Raffles nodded. 'I concur,' he said thoughtfully. 'If one of the great imperial powers were to march into his lands and take over, and that is quite likely these days, then they would leave him with little or nothing, perhaps not even his life. This way, he will be exchanging a share of his wealth for security, protection. As long as he chooses his partners wisely, he will be safe. There will be wealth in plenty.'

'Plenty for everybody?'

He laughed. 'I'll not deny that I have that at the back of my mind. The real question is, when best to act? I tend to think that delay is the best policy, for if I were signing an agreement of the sort we have postulated, I should make sure to have some payment on account, as it were.'

'Ah, but suppose that payment is only paper, banker's drafts, Bank of England notes, or what have you?'

Raffles shook his head. 'Mazawa is not your retiring, conservative City gent, Bunny. I take it you haven't run into him yet? No? Well, he wears a heavy gold bracelet on each wrist, diamond rings in profusion, and — when he wears his native dress — an enormous gold chain around his neck. Hangs almost to his waist.' He paused. 'And that's another thing — I said he sometimes wears native dress, a sort of long nightgown thing. I was talking to old 'Froggie' Phelps, he's in the Diplomatic Service, as you know, and he reckoned the costume was that of Nigeria, not the more easterly regions from whence Mazawa is reputed to hail.' He frowned. 'Another little mystery.'

★ ★ ★

The day after this conversation, I woke suddenly to find Raffles standing by my bed, his face flushed with anger. 'Have you read this?' he cried, waving a copy of the morning paper at me.

'Hardly!' said I, not without some ire. 'I was sound asleep, Raffles.'

He subsided slightly. 'My apologies for disturbing your much-needed beauty sleep, old chap, but this really is too much! We were talking yesterday of Chief Mazawa, and here he is in the paper this very morning. Do you know who he is thinking of signing an agreement with?'

'Is that entirely grammatical, I wonder? No,' I added hastily as Raffles advanced upon me, 'no, I don't know. Who, then?'

'Nathaniel Prout.'

'Oh, Lord!' I sat up in bed at this. 'Are you sure?' Raffles nodded, and I knew then why he had so rudely disturbed me. This Nathaniel Prout was the head of one of the larger mining concerns then operating out of London and into Africa. His nickname was 'Black Nat,' and this had several nuances of meaning, one of which was that, like the insect of a very similar name, he was a dratted nuisance. But there was another meaning, and that more sinister. Prout had an antipathy to anyone whose skin was darker than his own; the naughty word at which I hinted at the opening of this tale was the least offensive word to be heard on his lips when he spoke of such people. It was not merely dislike; I verily believe that he had some mental kink on the subject, that he truly believed the coloured races to be less than human, and treated them accordingly. As I say, the bulk of his mining operations were in foreign lands and used native labour, and he was reputed to treat these labourers worse than slaves. A fine sort of partner, this, for poor old Mazawa!

'Evidently Mazawa does not know Prout,' I stammered.

'Evidently.'

'But — ' I tried to collect my scattered wits together. 'But Prout must know Mazawa, or at least know of him. Why on earth is he, with his atrocious views, doing business — '

'Greed,' said Raffles shortly. 'Prout's lust for profit is temporarily overcoming his antipathy to men like Mazawa. Temporarily, and perhaps only apparently.'

'He means to cheat him?' I shook my head. 'Silly question, of course he does!'

Raffles nodded. 'And perhaps worse, for once Prout has his own men in the place, those armed guards which we — and Mazawa, I have no doubt — thought would be a useful asset, once they have marched in with Martini rifles and the like, then I for one wouldn't give much for Mazawa's life.'

'Lord, yes! You're right there. The poor fellow will be thrown out, if he isn't shot out of hand! What can we do, though?'

'We can warn Mazawa, if nothing else.

I hate to think of him falling into Prout's clutches, Bunny.'

I could not hide a smile at this. Here was Raffles, who had been happily speaking twenty-four hours ago of robbing Mazawa, wanting to keep him out of Prout's hands! 'A Christian duty, in fact,' I said. 'Or perhaps a Voodoo duty, in this case?'

Raffles regarded me seriously. 'You young ass! I tell you this, Bunny, if the fellow danced stark naked before the Prince of Darkness at each full moon, I should do all I could to save him from this villain, Prout. Come along, get dressed. And you haven't much time for breakfast, either.'

★ ★ ★

Chief Mazawa was, as you might expect, staying at one of the largest and grandest hotels in London. The receptionist looked a touch askance at us — even us! — as we stood there; indeed, I fancy that it was only the name of AJ Raffles which worked the trick at last. 'Monsieur Mazawa,' said the receptionist — using the same ridiculous convention as the 'Times' uses for foreign potentates — 'Monsieur Mazawa does not, as a rule, like to be disturbed much before noon. However, in this instance . . . ' and he waved to one of the pageboys to take us up.

Chief Mazawa was up, just, and we discovered him clad in silk pyjamas of a rather nice old rose shade, and a silk dressing gown in what I think is called eau-de-nil; a sort of pale blueish green. He was taking his breakfast, but stood up as we were announced, and waved us to chairs. 'Have you breakfasted, gentlemen? A glass of champagne, perhaps? Caviare?' His English was good, but not particularly well-bred; I fancied I caught more than a hint of Cockney, as a matter of fact. I thought that perhaps it was the result of his learning the language from Rhodesian or South African merchants, or something of the kind.

'A glass of — ' I began, but Raffles curtly silenced me with a wave of the hand.

'We shall not disturb you unduly, sir,' my friend began. 'The fact is, we have just read of your intentions with regard to the mineral wealth of your country, and we have come to offer what I hope is a timely word of advice.'

Chief Mazawa raised one eyebrow in a magnificent gesture of wonder. 'I have heard of you, of course, Mr Raffles,' said he, 'but always in connection with the game of cricket. It is on the field — pitch, I beg your pardon — that you are best known, is that not so?'

'Yes, but — '

'Are you perhaps also a business man, Mr Raffles? If so, then I confess I have not heard of you in that particular connection. But then, I have only just arrived in your beautiful country, so I am not at all well acquainted with everyone in Society and the world of commerce.'

'I make no claim to be a business man, sir,' said Raffles with dignity, carefully making 'business' and 'man' two separate words, and emphasizing the 'business' part of it, 'but I am a man, a human being, that is to say, and it distresses me to see you being fooled by this man Prout.'

Mazawa's eyebrow shot up again. 'Indeed? I fear that your meaning escapes me, Mr Raffles.'

'Then I shall make it clear to your Excellency. I believe — nay, I know — I know Nathaniel Prout to be a rogue, a man who will undoubtedly cheat you out of your money, and perhaps out of your life. Can I say plainer than that?'

Mazawa waved a hand airily. 'I have had long discussions with Mr Prout, and I have satisfied myself that he is genuine.'

Raffles sighed. 'Have you at the very least consulted a legal man, had him present during these discussions?'

Another wave of the hand, and, 'No, sir, I have not. It is unnecessary, quite unnecessary. My people are simple, unsophisticated. Honest. And I flatter myself that I am the same; more, that I am a good judge of character.'

'Well, sir, if you think that Prout is also an honest man, then I fear that you are deluding yourself,' said Raffles shortly.

Mazawa stood up. 'I am sure that you are acting from the very best of motives, Mr Raffles, but I assure you that I am well able to look after myself.'

'Then there is nothing more to be said, sir. We shall not trouble you further.' Raffles picked up his hat, rose to take his leave, then hesitated. 'You would not consider having a friend — or at any rate someone who has your interests at heart — present at the negotiations?'

'Quite unnecessary, I assure you.' Mazawa made as if to reach for the bell.

'We can see ourselves out.' Again Raffles turned, and again he hesitated. 'Would it be a great impertinence to ask what form the negotiations will take? What stage they have reached?'

Mazawa frowned, as if he failed to understand the point of the question, but he answered readily enough. 'There is no secret about it, Mr Raffles. I am to meet Mr Prout at his office this very afternoon. We shall sign the necessary documents, and he is to pay me an earnest — is that the word? A little something on account, against future royalties.'

'Again, is it in order to ask, what form is this 'earnest' of his good intentions to take? A banker's draft, perhaps?'

Mazawa grinned broadly at this. 'Oh, dear me, no! Diamonds, Mr Raffles, diamonds from his mines in southern Africa. And rubies from Ceylon, or some such place.'

'May I venture to suggest an independent appraisal?'

Mazawa nodded, more seriously. 'You may be sure that I have thought of all that is going through your mind, Mr Raffles. I shall take an expert, the assistant manager of one of the largest jewellers in London,' and he mentioned the name of the firm. 'Nothing will be signed, by me at any rate, before his opinion has been delivered.'

Raffles smiled. 'That, at least, is wise,' he said simply. He shook Mazawa's hand, and we left.

As we reached the street, Raffles said, 'I'm glad he's taking old Huntley along,' — meaning the jeweller, who was, of course, known to us both in what I might loosely term a professional capacity. 'He, at least, is honest as the day is long.'

'Still,' said I, wondering, 'odd that he should want diamonds, Raffles. I thought he was dripping with them to begin with?'

'A man cannot have too many diamonds, Bunny,' said Raffles. But his tone did not reflect the lightness of his words. He went on slowly, sounding almost as if it were himself that he was trying to convince, 'It may be that rumour has it wrong, that there are no diamonds in Mazawa's lands. Again, diamonds are portable wealth, are they not? Money, a lot of it, in a small compass, and money is always useful.' He shook his head. 'But it's deuced odd, none the less. Not a very satisfactory way of doing business. No — ' and he stopped in his tracks, and stared at me.

I seldom had Raffles puzzled — usually it was the other way round! — and I pursued my advantage. 'Had it not been that Huntley was going along, I'd have guessed that Prout would foist Mazawa off with fakes.'

Raffles gripped my arm, so tightly that I gasped. 'By Heaven, Bunny, that's what he is going to do!' he said.

'And Huntley?'

'Oh, Huntley's honest enough, as we've

just agreed. No, Prout will let Huntley examine the stones and certify as to their genuine nature. But then, when once the documents are signed and sealed, Prout will ply Mazawa with drink, or something of that sort, and find a way to switch the stones. I'm as sure of that as I am that today's Tuesday!'

I frowned. 'And what exactly is the purpose of this postulated deception? I mean, I know it would cheat Mazawa in the short term, but what would Prout's ultimate object be? After all, when — if — Mazawa were to find out that he'd been fobbed off with fakes, then he could simply repudiate the contract he'd signed with Prout!'

'Ah, but could he? You may be sure, Bunny, that Prout will make very certain that the contract is iron-clad, rock solid, or whatever metaphor your literary mind might suggest. Once Mazawa has signed, there will be no withdrawing from it. As to why Prout should cheat him at this stage, I can think of several possible reasons.'

'Such as?'

'Well, such as the fact that, although Mazawa will have seen the diamonds and rubies that he is to receive — or that he thinks he is to receive — Prout has not, unless he is better informed than you or I or the hundreds of others who take an interest in Mazawa, Prout has not actually seen any of Mazawa's wealth, from that 'remote' kingdom, apart from the gold Mazawa wears about his person.'

I nodded to show that I followed him.

Raffles went on, 'Now, Prout, unpleasant though he undoubtedly is, has not got where he is today by being gullible. Prout will reason that he has not seen any gold, diamonds, or what have you, from Mazawa's lands; and Prout will not buy a pig in a poke. In fairness, and if it were anyone but Prout, one could see the sense in that. Suppose that Mazawa's gold mine contains only what he has about him? It's possible, quite possible. Mazawa would have the diamonds — assuming, as always, that he actually gets them, and that they are not fakes — but would be giving nothing in return.'

'But I don't see why Mazawa would do

that. I mean to say, I can see that he might want to cheat Prout, or whoever he was to sign the agreement with, but then — oh, I see! Mazawa clears out, leaves his people to explain that there's nothing left. Yes, I see.'

Raffles nodded. 'Let me put yet another possibility before you. Suppose that Mazawa has no wealth, but that he has a rival, or rivals; a brother, perhaps, who has challenged him for the chieftainship, or an enemy tribe which is poised to invade. Would a hundred heavily armed soldiers of fortune not be a useful asset, even if they were there only long enough to eliminate one's enemies?'

'Yes, an interesting point. But what of Prout? Even if he cheats Mazawa at this stage, then he must still pay his soldiers of fortune, his mining engineers and what have you, whether or not he finds gold or diamonds there. He won't be best pleased if there isn't anything after all!'

'No, and that is precisely why he means to cut his possible losses by cheating Mazawa! As to his paying his men, they would be there anyway; all Prout would lose is a week's salary for them — a reasonable amount, perhaps, but no vast fortune. And remember that even if Mazawa has no mineral wealth, he still has his people, his tribe.'

I thought for a moment. 'You mean that Prout would enslave them? Come on, Raffles, this is the end of the nineteenth century!'

'And how long since the American war was fought over the same issue? If some of the tales coming from Brazil, and from the Congo, are to be believed, slavery is still very much with us, Bunny. No, Prout would be sure to salvage something from the worst situation. As a final point for your consideration, Prout's monstrous outlook, his abominable prejudices, would prevent his dealing squarely with anyone like Mazawa under any circumstances.'

'Well, we seem to have covered a good many possibilities!' I said with an attempt at a smile.

'We do indeed.'

'But we still don't know anything for sure?'

'That is true in a sense,' said Raffles

thoughtfully. 'I don't know just what is wrong about this whole business, but I'd stake my life that something is wrong. I can feel it, Bunny.'

'Raffles — ' I hesitated.

'Yes, Bunny?'

'Oh, nothing. What I should have asked was, assuming that your worst suspicions are correct, then what, if anything, can we do about it?'

He shook his head. 'There you have me, Bunny. If the fellow won't let me help him, what the devil can I do?' He thought for a moment. 'It might perhaps be permissible, having spoken to him this morning, to return this evening and check whether the signing and sealing did indeed go without any sort of hitch. Could we do that, Bunny? I rather think we might. That would at least reassure resolve the matter one way or the other, and we can consider our next actions accordingly.'

'You think you may possibly have done the man Prout an injustice, then?'

'Say, rather, that I suspect that I may have underestimated Mazawa. I thought at first that he must be that simple, unsophisticated creature he claims to be, but I'm not sure. He has a head on his shoulders, and I have a sneaking suspicion that he may yet prove a match for Prout. If that's so, then I shall withdraw, and not interfere again.' And he set off at a good pace, and would not answer any of the questions which I put to him.

At the hour when honest folk are thinking of taking their tea, Raffles and I returned to Mazawa'a hotel. The same receptionist, almost effusive this time, had us shown up. Mazawa was drinking champagne, just as he had done at breakfast — he must, I reflected with some envy, have a head like cast iron! — and this time when he offered us a glass, I did not allow Raffles to refuse for me, although he himself declined.

'Come to give me more valuable business advice, Mr Raffles?' said Mazawa, not unkindly.

'In a way, sir. I merely wondered — believe me, I have only your best interests at heart when I ask it — but I wondered if all had gone well with your enterprise?'

Mazawa waved a large hand in an airy gesture. 'If you still harbour that ridiculous notion about the stones, Mr Raffles, then you can forget it! Mr Huntley assures me that they are genuine, and of the best quality, and in every way acceptable.'

'H'mm.' I could see that Raffles was nonplussed, but he went on, 'I am sure you are right, sir. But I wonder, would it be a very great impertinence to ask to see the stones?'

The merest hint of a frown clouded Mazawa's cheerful countenance. 'I fear I do not actually have the stones, Mr Raffles.'

'Ah!'

Mazawa waved his hand again, impatiently this time. 'No, no, it is not what you think. There was something wrong with the contract, an important clause had inadvertently been omitted. The fault of Mr Prout's secretary. He called the poor fellow in and — what is the phrase? — hauled him over the coals. Indeed, I felt almost sorry for the poor chap, even though he had caused me some inconvenience and delay. But I am assured that the contract will be duly amended by tomorrow — a heavy night's work for the poor secretary, I fear! And I am to return tomorrow, first thing, and sign my name accordingly.'

'Will you take Mr Huntley with you again?'

Mazawa frowned. 'I see no need for that, Mr Raffles. It was, of course, merely good business to check the stones in the first place, but to ask to check them again would be to cast aspersions on Mr Prout's honesty. Mr Prout locked them in his safe as I watched, and there they will remain until tomorrow, when the revised agreement is signed.'

'H'mm,' said Raffles through his nose. Then he shrugged his shoulders, smiled, and held out his hand to Mazawa. 'Well, sir, we have taken up too much of your valuable time already. It merely remains for me to wish you well of your bargain.'

I echoed this sentiment, feeling rather sorry in my own mind that I had only had time for the one glass of champagne. Almost before I knew where I was, we were out in the street.

'Well!' said Raffles, angrily. 'I thought it as well to leave, otherwise my temper would have got the better of me. I thought I had underestimated him, but I see I was wrong! The man's a complete fool! He evidently doesn't see what's in front of his face.'

'The stones have been switched, of course?'

Raffles nodded. 'Or they will be, by the time Mazawa receives them. And that being so, there's only one thing we can do.'

'Go to dinner, see a show, and forget the whole thing?'

'Go to an early dinner, certainly, for it's not dark enough yet for the second part of the evening's entertainment. Which is not, by the way, exactly what you have just suggested.'

'Somehow,' said I, 'I knew it wouldn't be!'

★ ★ ★

Prout's offices were on the top floor of an imposing block in the City. There was a night watchman, of sorts, but I can testify that he was earning his wages under false pretences. Raffles and I eluded the fellow without the least difficulty, and made our way up to Prout's private office.

'There's the safe,' said Raffles, nodding at a large and very indifferent portrait in oils of Prout himself that hung behind the desk. 'I only hope he hasn't taken the real stones away with him!'

He set to work on the safe, and I began glancing in a desultory way through the various drawers of the desk. They contained the usual miscellanea of a businessman's life, with the sole exception of one which I could not open, though I tried Raffles' skeleton keys on it. 'Raffles?'

'Shh!' By that time he had the safe open, and was going through the contents. He looked at me with some consternation. 'Damn the man!'

'And why, pray?'

Raffles held up a little wash-leather bag. 'These are pretty clearly the fakes, which he hopes to foist upon Mazawa — I'll check them in a moment to make sure. But I had thought — hoped — that the real stones would be here as well, and they're not. Prout has evidently taken them away with him.'

'Perhaps not,' I said, as lightly as I could manage. 'There's a drawer here which I cannot open.'

'Oh?' Raffles turned his attention to the desk. 'Here's a thing, Bunny! Pass me those tools, would you?'

The safe had taken some ten minutes to open; the desk drawer took a full five and twenty. When it was open, we could see why it had presented such difficulties, for the lock was as complicated as any safe mechanism I have ever seen, while the drawer itself was lined with hardened steel, a good inch thick. The whole drawer was effectively a small safe in itself.

Raffles pulled out of the drawer a second wash-leather bag.

'The real stones?' I hazarded.

'I imagine so.' He took out his eyeglass and studied the stones closely. 'Yes, as we thought. The stones in the drawer are the real ones, the ones which Mazawa and Huntley examined. Those in the safe are fakes — excellent fakes, by the way, and I suspect that even I would not have spotted them if my suspicions had not been aroused to begin with. A superficial glance will convince Mazawa that the fakes are real, he will sign away his birthright, and . . . ' and he shrugged expressively.

'The question now — and it's a question I started to ask earlier and didn't — is, what are we to do?'

'Ah! You ask a question to which I have no ready answer, Bunny. I have been, as it were, plunged headlong into this whole business, and had no time to formulate a plan of campaign.'

'If we swapped the stones, then Mazawa would have the real ones, at least,' I elaborated. 'But then Prout would be sure to take out the fakes, which he would think were real, to gloat over them. He would spot the switch, and take action against Mazawa, have him bumped off, like as not!'

' 'Bumped off', Bunny? Dear me! And you a writer! But you're quite right,' added Raffles thoughtfully. 'And even if by some chance Mazawa got away with the stones, he would still have signed his country, his mineral wealth and — worst of all — his people, over to the tender mercies of this beast Prout.'

'And it's not even as if we could pinch the stones outright,' I went on gloomily. 'Prout would simply get new ones, and new fakes, and go through the whole business again. Indeed, stealing the stones might make matters worse, for Mazawa would think that no thief would bother to steal fakes! He'd be even less suspicious of Prout next time round, so we should effectively have been assisting Prout!'

'H'mm. You sum up our predicament neatly, Bunny.' Raffles thought for a moment, then laughed aloud. He took one of the little bags and replaced it in the drawer. 'There, Bunny. Those are the fakes, but if we close and lock the drawer — so! — Prout will think they are the real stones, and that the crooks were fooled, or defeated, by his secret drawer.' He stood up. 'I shall retain the real stones, and leave the safe door ajar, thus. Now, Prout or his people will see that tomorrow, and very naturally assume that he has been the victim of a robbery. A singularly unsuccessful robbery, Prout will go on to assume, for, so far as Prout knows, the crooks have taken the fake stones!'

'Amusing enough, Raffles,' I said with a frown, 'but I confess that the purpose rather eludes me.'

'Well, Prout is hardly going to hand the real stones — or, rather, what he believes to be the real stones — over to Mazawa, is he? He will beat his breast, show the open safe, ask for time to acquire new stones.'

'Thereby deferring the day of signature of this monstrous agreement?'

'As you say. I only hope that I can use the breathing space to convince Mazawa to take some elementary precautions, even if I cannot persuade him to find another partner altogether. If necessary, I'll tell Mazawa about Prout's scheme with the stones, insist that Huntley sees them on the very day of signature.'

Another idea had struck me. 'And suppose that Prout has an access of conscience, and hands over what he believes to be the real stones?'

Raffles thought, then laughed silently. 'Even better if he did, Bunny! I should visit Mazawa again, ask to see them, frown, and suggest consulting Huntley. He would confirm the stones to be fakes, and Prout's whole scheme would be ruined.'

I thought in my turn. 'But then why not just suggest that Huntley check the stones anyway? We tried that, and Mazawa wouldn't listen. The whole essence of a confidence trick is the confidence; the victim must have confidence in the trickster, and Mazawa has — Lord only knows why! — confidence in Prout! He just wouldn't take any notice of us. And even if he did, the damage would be done, the contract would have been signed, and Prout would claim that he had given Mazawa real stones, in good faith. Most likely he would pretend that Mazawa had switched them himself, to make trouble, or something of the kind. You yourself said that Prout would make sure that Mazawa could not get out of the contract, come what may.'

'H'mm.' I have seldom known Raffles

at much of a loss for words, but he was puzzled now. After a lengthy pause, he said, 'I take your point, Bunny. But I do not think it is a serious objection, for I cannot see the man Prout handing over stones which he believes to be genuine.' He thought a moment longer, then I got the distinct impression that he shrugged his shoulders, though it was too dark for me to be sure. 'In any case, Bunny, I really cannot see what more we can do. We have tried our best, and can console ourselves with that knowledge, whatever the outcome may be.'

★　★　★

The outcome was somewhat unexpected. I had gone round to Raffles' rooms on the following day, in the hope of being a spectator in the curious drama that was unfolding. I had barely settled in an armchair and lit a cigar when there was a tremendous commotion in the corridor outside, and a pounding at the door.

Raffles and I gazed at one another with a wild surmise. 'Mackenzie?' I stuttered.

'I — ' It was only for a moment that he was agitated, then Raffles, with a superhuman effort, became his old, calm self. 'Get the door, would you, Bunny?' As I rose, Raffles also got to his feet and moved silently to a cupboard. I assumed that the stones were hidden therein, and that he wished to be nearer to them in case of emergency; though what he hoped to salvage from this, I could not imagine.

With great trepidation I opened the door, and was immediately brushed aside. It was not our old adversary Inspector Mackenzie, but Mazawa himself, his face distorted with fury, who pushed past me into the room. 'Have you got those stones?' he demanded without preamble.

'Will your Excellency not take a seat? Perhaps a cigar? Or — '

'The stones, Mr Raffles!' Mazawa had settled down slightly, but he moved closer to Raffles, and his great fists clenched in a menacing fashion.

'It seems useless to pretend that I have no idea what your Excellency means, so I will ask only this: how did you know to come here, to me?'

Mazawa permitted himself a grim little smile. 'You showed such a keen interest in my business dealings, Mr Raffles. And in the stones, of course. And then I have heard your name, not in connection with your performance upon the cricket field, but in quite another context. Oh, nothing that can be proved, you understand. Rumours, hints, a shrug of the shoulders here, a raised eyebrow there, but the sort of thing that an intelligent man can weave theories around.'

'I see. You have not by any chance mentioned these — theories — to anyone?'

'The police, you mean?' Mazawa laughed aloud. 'No, Mr Raffles, you need have no fear of that! That is, as long as I get those stones back immediately.'

'I assure your Excellency that I had only your best interests at heart.'

Mazawa nodded. 'I am convinced of that. Were I not, I should have brought an inspector from Scotland Yard along with me.'

I shuddered involuntarily, but managed to ask, 'What will you tell Prout, sir? I mean, how will you account for having recovered the stones so quickly?'

Mazawa dismissed this with a wave of the hand. 'I shall say that I had a clue, an anonymous letter, that I paid for information and for the return of the stones. I think that Mr Prout will be so glad to see them again that he will not ask for details.'

'I think you are right,' said Raffles. He took a little bag from the cupboard, and handed it to Mazawa. 'Will you check the stones, sir?'

Mazawa shook his head. 'I trust you, Mr Raffles. And now, if you will excuse me . . . ' and he was gone before either of us could add anything.

Raffles stood for a long time gazing at the door, and then he turned to me and spread his arms in a theatrical gesture of resignation. 'What can one say, Bunny?'

'Well, at least Mazawa will get the real stones, Raffles!'

'At least? Well put, Bunny, for he will get nothing else, if I know Prout. And even then — ' and he broke off abruptly and strode to the hat stand. 'Come along, Bunny.'

'Where to?'

'To Prout's office. Oh, only to wait outside,' he added with a laugh, as my face fell. 'I want to be sure that Mazawa has those stones. 'At least', as you put it.'

We took a cab and waited outside Prout's office. After an hour or so, the uniformed doorman snapped to attention, and Chief Mazawa, in a natty grey business suit, came out into the street. He was grinning like the proverbial Cheshire cat, and the doorman's face also lit up as Mazawa gave him what was evidently a generous tip.

Before the doorman could look for a cab, Raffles had got down and held open the door of our own vehicle. I could have sworn that Mazawa's face showed a touch of apprehension as he saw us, but perhaps it was merely surprise — unless, thought I, he suspects that we still have designs on his precious stones!

'May we offer your Excellency a lift?' Raffles was saying.

Mazawa hesitated, then got into our cab.

'Where to, gents?' asked the cabbie.

Raffles looked at Mazawa, who said, 'I am bound for Charing Cross.'

'Indeed? Charing Cross, cabbie!' And Raffles regarded Mazawa with some interest. 'Leaving the country, your Excellency?'

'Oh, just a little jaunt to the Continent. Paris, Berlin, you know,' said Mazawa vaguely.

'And would it be in order to ask if everything went to plan this time? No paragraphs missing from the agreement, or anything of that kind?'

Mazawa gave a great laugh, of relief as it seemed to me. 'No, Mr Raffles, everything was as it should be.'

'I wonder — may I perhaps see the stones once more?'

Mazawa frowned, but then his face cleared. 'Of course.' He took the little bag from an inside pocket, and passed it to Raffles.

Raffles produced his lens, and glanced at one or two of the stones before replacing them in the bag and handing it back to Mazawa. 'Thank you, your Excellency.'

'Rather fine, are they not?'

'They are indeed.'

'And now perhaps you will agree that you have mistaken Mr Prout's motives and intentions?'

I think that Raffles must have had some difficulty in biting back the caustic retort that came unbidden to his lips. But he did it like a man, saying merely, 'I am pleased that things seem to be satisfactory, your Excellency.'

Curious, I asked, 'Did Prout not query your finding the stones, sir?'

'As I told you,' said Mazawa, 'I said that I had paid for their return and Mr Prout was not disposed to take the matter further. Indeed, so heartened was he to see them again that he positively insisted on reimbursing me what I had paid! As I had not actually paid anything, it was a touch embarrassing, but I claimed to have laid out five hundred pounds, and Mr Prout happily dispensed that amount in notes.' And he reinforced the point by taking out a thick wad of paper, and waving it in the air. 'I am grateful to you, Mr Raffles, and to you, Mr Manders, for your concern. I shall not insult you by offering you any of this money, but you have my sincere thanks.'

'Oh, you wouldn't — ' I began, but Raffles waved me to silence, seeming inclined to speak himself.

Before he could, though, Mazawa had slipped a heavy gold bracelet from his wrist, and handed it to Raffles. 'A memento, Mr Raffles. As I say, I am grateful to you.'

'Thank you, your Excellency. May I urge caution, however, in any further dealings with Prout?'

'Oh, you may be sure that I shall watch my step!' Mazawa laughed, then nodded at the window. 'Here we are, I see. Gentlemen, I thank you once again. It is unlikely that we shall meet again, but it has been a pleasure. Most instructive.' And he was down from the cab and lost in the throng round the station before we could make any proper reply.

'The Albany, cabbie,' called Raffles, and then he sank down and relapsed into a sort of gloomy silence.

'Not one of our triumphs, Raffles?' I

ventured, but he merely grunted.

As we went into the Albany, the porter called to Raffles. 'Beg pardon, Mr Raffles, but there's a gentleman called to see you.'

'Oh?'

The porter frowned. 'Well, sir, I say 'gentleman' — a professor, sir. I put him in your rooms.'

Raffles glanced at me and led the way upstairs. The professor who had been left in his rooms like any parcel was a tall, thin man, with a vague expression. 'Ah,' said Raffles, 'Professor Morton-Pyke,' and he made the necessary introductions. 'Is it about Chief Mazawa?' he then asked.

'It is, sir. I was intrigued by your questions, and looked into the matter, with some interesting results.'

'Mazawa is a fraud?' said Raffles.

Morton-Pyke looked shocked. 'You put the matter bluntly, sir, and most unscientifically. But still, having regard to all the information germane to the case, I am bound to say that your recapitulation is not entirely unfounded in actuality.'

To my credit, I worked this out a fraction of a second before Raffles. 'You mean he is a fraud?'

'In a word, yes.'

'No mysterious central African tribe, then?' asked Raffles.

'No.'

'No chieftain?'

'No.'

'Above all, no vast mineral wealth?'

'I have not the facts as to that,' said Professor Morton-Pyke severely, 'but in view of the circumstances, one rather surmises not.'

'But then what is the fellow? Who is he?' I wanted to know.

Morton-Pyke shook his head. 'There we must enter the realms of pure speculation, sir. I can tell you where he comes from, though. Or at any rate, where he learned his English.'

'Can you, though?' asked Raffles.

Morton-Pyke nodded. 'When you first approached me, I had not heard him speak, of course. But, as I say, my curiosity was piqued, and I made it my business to scrape some acquaintance with him. Only a few moments, you are to understand, but then I have something of a reputation — if I may go so far! — as an expert on these matters.' And he smiled complacently.

With an obvious effort, Raffles remained calm. 'And?'

'And? Oh, indeed. Yes, he undoubtedly learned his English from a sailor, or sailors. And he has spent some time in the Portugese colonial town of Lourenço Marques. The more — ah, insalubrious area, I should add.'

I said, 'You mean the red — ' but Raffles cast me a glance which silenced me.

Morton-Pyke went on, 'Based upon this information, and given the size of Mr Mazawa — if such I may style him — I should judge that he was formerly a stoker on a tramp steamer. Or something on very much the same lines,' he added with the usual academic reluctance to be too specific.

'A stoker on a tramp steamer, eh?' said Raffles thoughtfully. Then he asked Morton-Pyke, 'Would you care for a drink, sir? A cigar?'

'Thank you, no. I must be off,' and he suited his actions to the words.

When the door had closed, I looked at Raffles. 'But, then —'

'Then Prout has been done, Bunny! Gloriously, magnificently, done! Done to a turn!' He smiled, and added, 'And so have we, for that bracelet is not gold!' He tossed it over to me. 'More your style than mine, anyway!'

I scratched my head. 'So Mazawa knew what was happening all along, then? He meant to swindle Prout, not the other way round?'

Raffles nodded. 'And he succeeded.'

'But only with our help,' I pointed out. 'Had you not switched those stones, Prout would not have gained anything, it's true, but no more would Mazawa.'

'That is quite true, Bunny, and I think it's something we can look upon with a touch of pardonable pride.'

'I suppose so,' said I churlishly. 'We've helped Mazawa make a dent in Prout's vast fortune, if you want to look at it in that light.'

'Oh, more than that, I fancy, Bunny. You see, when it comes out that Mazawa was a fraud, then Prout's reputation will take a knock. But then he will try to claim that he knew the truth all along, and fobbed Mazawa off with fake stones! He will parade the real ones for all to see, to show how clever he, Prout, is.'

'But they're not the real stones, Raffles!'

'Just so. Think about it for a moment, Bunny. When Prout tries to sell the stones, it will all come out! Oh, he will try to make a brave show, to hide it, but these things cannot be hidden. Especially if some-one or the other puts a rumour about, of course,' he added thoughtfully. 'And the City is an unforgiving sort of place, you know. Once let something like this happen, show that you can be fooled, that you have lost your grip, and people will think twice about doing business with you! I should not be at all surprised if this is not the beginning of the end for Mr Prout.'

'So,' I said, 'that may or may not happen. Meantime, Mazawa has some rather fine jewels, and five hundred in cash, to blow in Paris in what one imagines is the traditional way in which stokers on tramp steamers do blow a small fortune in Paris! Lucky devil! I have a showy, if imitation, bracelet. What have you got, Raffles?'

'Merely the knowledge that justice has been done, Bunny. And that, I fear, must suffice for me. Not one of our best efforts, as you yourself observed,' he added, lighting a Sullivan, 'but one cannot, as they say, win them all.'

'Indeed not, Raffles.' I stood up. 'A brandy and soda, perhaps? To drown our sorrows and drink Mazawa's health?'

'Both acceptable and appropriate, Bunny. Oh, I almost forgot — there is one other little thing I have gleaned from all this,' he added, as I busied myself with tantalus and gasogene.

'Oh?'

For answer, he held up a little slip of wax; and I knew without being told that it was the impression of the lock in Prout's secret drawer.

None the less, I frowned. 'But the diamonds in there are fake!'

'True,' said Raffles. 'But the drawer held more than just fake diamonds. A great deal more, Bunny. Are you free this evening?'

7

THE READ POETS SOCIETY

It was not often that AJ Raffles came round to my humble abode in Mount Street; as a general rule, it was I who went to visit him in his rooms in the Albany. On this particular morning in the year 1892, however, I was finishing my breakfast when Raffles came drifting into my tiny establishment like the oily yellow fog of early December which crept along the London streets.

'Hullo!' I said, somewhat surprised to see him so early, and equally surprised at the gloomy expression on his face. 'How are things? I must say, you look considerably less than sprightly.'

He gave a shrug far removed from his habitual cheery smile. 'Ennui, Bunny. Or, if you prefer, le cafard. Boredom, if you insist on the plain word.' He certainly seemed unsettled, wandering round my sitting room, picking up the various paltry ornaments and putting them down again. 'Curse this fog!' he exclaimed suddenly. 'And this darkness; and this cold! Would that it were spring, and the invitations to cricket parties arriving by each post!'

'Ah, so that's it, is it?' I said. 'Well, in that case, have a cup of coffee and a bite to eat, for I may just have a little something here which will interest you.' And I threw across the solitary letter which was all my morning post. 'Read it, if you like.'

Raffles, still in downhearted mood, frowned at the envelope, then held it under his nose. 'A woman, Bunny? Hidden depths — ' and he broke off as he took out the half sheet of notepaper. 'Oh! Mr James Emerson. I beg his pardon.' And he sniffed the paper again, in a rather patronizing fashion, but, I was pleased to note, with much of his old gaiety.

'A man's cologne is a matter for his own conscience, you know, Raffles,' I murmured.

'Just so, Bunny. 'I am the Secretary of

the Read Poets Society — ',' he frowned, then smiled, 'Oh, I see. It's pronounced 'Reed', of course, the village being Little Read, as I see now that I look at the address.' He glanced at me. 'A charming spot, Bunny.'

'You know the place, then?'

'I've visited the village, though I never heard of an 'Emerson's',' said Raffles vaguely. 'Some historical thing, I can't quite recall the details.' Before I could ask what, if anything, he meant by that, he went on, 'I suppose they don't use the full place-name because it would seem to anyone not in the know as if it were 'The Little-read Poets Society', and no poet would want to risk that! Let us see — 'Emerson's, Little Read: Dear Mr Manders — I am the Secretary of the Read Poets Society, and am writing to ask if you might favour the Society with a reading of some of your work next weekend. I regret that the small size of our Society precludes any sort of fee, but I myself can offer you a bed, a humble table, and some respectable claret. Please feel free to bring your wife, or other companion, along. Do come! Yours, et cetera, James Emerson'. H'mm. 'Wife, or other companion', I see. Rather bohemian, that, Bunny!'

'You silly ass! But — respectable claret, Raffles! Could you get away? Would you?'

'Oh, certainly, certainly. No other engagements, Bunny.' He sniffed the paper again, and then held it close to his eyes and looked at it carefully. 'A woman wrote this, you know.'

'Surely not? The signature — '

'Oh, not the signature, that's a man. H'mm — steady enough, although written with some effort, I'd say. But the rest of it is written by a woman — you yourself noticed the perfume — yes, and a masterful woman at that. And related to the man who signed it, too. The Greek 'e', the loop on the top of the 'r', both quite conclusive. There are seventeen other points of similarity, with which I shall not bore you. You did not notice the two different hands? No, of course not; that demonstrates how very close they are. His daughter, I imagine, Miss Emerson.'

'She may be married, Raffles?'

'In that case, how comes she to be still at home, writing letters for her father? No, Miss Emerson it is, I fancy.'

★ ★ ★

I scribbled a reply to Mr Emerson, and in turn received a note to the effect the he regretted that he had no carriage, but that 'Emerson's,' the house, was at no great walking distance from the railway. And on the following Friday Raffles and I alighted at the tiny 'halt on demand' station of Little Read. The weather had turned colder, and there were odd flakes of snow drifting past. I turned up my coat collar and shivered. 'Hope it isn't too far, Raffles! I thought you said this was a charming spot?'

Raffles, by now his cheerful old self, laughed. 'It is, in June, Bunny. Which is when I was here last.' He waved an arm at the fields and hedges along the little lane, now turning grey with the approaching darkness and a dusting of snow. 'The village is five minutes away,' he added, lifting his bag from the tiny wooden platform and setting off with a confident stride.

After a couple of minutes we saw the first cottages, and Raffles hailed a passing farm labourer, homeward bound for his supper, and asked where 'Emerson's' might be.

The labourer scratched his head. 'Mr Emerson, is it? That'd be the big house, stands on its own down that way,' and he pointed. 'Used to be called 'The Elms',' he added helpfully.

'Ah,' said Raffles, 'It was called 'The Elms' when I was last here. Yes, I know it. Thank you,' and off he went again. 'It was the name that threw me off the scent,' he explained as we walked along. 'This fellow Emerson evidently changed the name when he moved in.'

I confess I rather sniffed at this, feeling that it smacked of arrogance; but before I could express my sentiments in words, Raffles had pointed at a large, old house, set in among a veritable grove of tall elm trees, clearly the origin of the house's former name. All the windows of the place were glowing with a light that betokened warmth and comfort. I shivered again, but with a sort of pleasurable anticipation this time, and quickened my pace.

The door was opened to us by a rather youthful but otherwise conventional enough butler, who showed us into a warm and well-lit sitting room. Our host, Mr James Emerson, was seated in an armchair, and did not rise to greet us. 'Forgive me, gentlemen,' he said, with a gesture at his legs. 'I fear that I do not get around as easily these days as I would wish.'

As I murmured the conventional platitudes, I covertly studied Mr Emerson. A man of fifty or so, not more, a good six feet in height, as I judged, but all too clearly suffering from the ravages of some wasting disease. His clothes hung loosely on his gaunt frame, and his face was like a death's head surmounted by a shock of pure white hair. A chair with wheels stood in a corner of the room, and would have told its own tale, even without Mr Emerson's appearance. Discreet as I flattered myself I had been, Mr Emerson evidently caught my glance, for he laughed and told me, 'It is by no means as painful as it might appear, Mr Manders. Merely inconvenient.'

Before I could think, I blurted out, 'And your doctors?'

Mr Emerson shook his head, but then raised a finger to his lips as the door opened, and an attractive woman of twenty or so came into the room. 'Ah, Letitia,' said Mr Emerson. 'Come and meet Mr Manders, and his friend Mr Raffles. Gentlemen, my daughter, Letitia, who acts as my housekeeper and secretary.'

Miss Emerson was, as I say, a most attractive young woman, with long dark hair. Her dark eyes had an anxious look, I assumed because she was concerned about her father's poor state of health. She greeted us civilly enough, but then said that she had much to attend to in the kitchen, and excused herself accordingly, saying that Galton, the butler, would bring us some tea and then show us to our rooms when once we had thawed out somewhat.

As we drank our tea, Mr Emerson said,

somewhat awkwardly, 'I have concealed the true state of affairs from my daughter, gentlemen. She knows that I am ill, of course, but not the full gravity of the illness. I think it the best way, and I should be obliged if you would respect my wishes and say nothing of the matter before her.'

Of course we agreed; I did not know just how Raffles might have felt, but I was most embarrassed. I had never met Mr Emerson before that afternoon, and here he was pouring his most intimate secrets out to me. Of course, I felt sorry for the man, more so than I could well express in words, and were there anything that I could have done to help, I'd have done it like a shot; but for all that it was an awkward sort of position to be put in, and I was glad when the butler showed Raffles and me up to our rooms.

When once Galton had left us, Raffles looked at me and raised an eyebrow, but said nothing.

'I say, Raffles! I'm most frightfully sorry about all this, you know. I really had no idea — '

He waved this aside. 'I feel bad about

our host, Bunny. I'm sure there is something more than he has told us, some trouble even worse than the obvious one.'

'You think so? Yes, now you mention it, for a man does not tell complete strangers of his worries in that way, not as a rule. That suggests that the obvious trouble is not what is really worrying him! That's it, Raffles!'

He nodded. 'Neatly put, Bunny. You know, I begin to think that it may have been a good thing, our coming down here.' And he smiled, and sought his own room.

Dinner was a curious meal. There were but the four of us, our host and his daughter, Raffles, myself. Mr Emerson explained, 'The Society is a small one, as I think my daughter's note said; indeed, there are but half a dozen of us. The rest are to come tomorrow, and the original intention was that they should leave in the evening, and return on Sunday — they all live quite close, of course, though mostly from outside the village itself, so they must travel a couple of miles or so.

Ordinarily that would be no trouble, but with this weather — ' and he gestured at the windows. Although the curtains were closed, the steady patter of snow driving against the glass could be heard clearly. 'Some of them may not turn out at all, but I've told them to bring night things if they do come, just in case,' Mr Emerson added with a smile, 'and so we might have a fairly large party for the whole weekend!'

Miss Letitia Emerson did not seem inclined to take any part in the conversation, and she excused herself almost as soon as the table had been cleared. Her father looked after her as the door closed, and sighed. He had refused more than a glass of his 'respectable claret' — and I may add that it was more than respectable — with the meal, saying that his doctors frowned upon it, but now he poured himself a decent glass of a fine old cognac, and as he sipped that he seemed to become more talkative.

'You gentlemen must excuse my telling you my troubles in that abrupt fashion,' he began. 'But the fact is, I see few new faces these days, and I cannot well talk to those people whom I do know well. Besides, I am pretty well past any notions of conventional behaviour now,' and he gave a bitter smile.

'What — exactly — ' I stammered out.

'What exactly is it? Something with a Latin name eight or nine syllables long; it would mean as little to you as it did to me — once upon a time! As I told you, Letitia knows I am unwell, knows some of my troubles, money and the like; but she does not know just how little time I have left. She is my only concern now, gentlemen; if I can see her married and settled, I can face the rest with relative ease.'

'You will forgive the observation, sir,' said Raffles, 'but I should have thought your daughter had no shortage of admirers?'

Mr Emerson smiled. 'Her own natural advantages are considerable, though perhaps it is not for me to say as much. But the snag is, she has no fortune.'

Raffles said nothing, but he glanced involuntarily at the bottles on the table, then shifted his gaze to take in the comfortable room as a whole.

'Ah,' said Mr Emerson, 'I see what you are thinking, Mr Raffles! But the cellar was laid down a few years ago, when I was still hale and hearty. Are you ready to hear the story of my life, I wonder? Very well. My family is an old one in these parts. This house was once ours, and it was then called 'Emerson's', the fashion round about here being to call the house after the family, as you may know. We were, I believe, landowners on a large scale at one time, although there are no written records to substantiate that particular old family tradition.

'Anyway, something — don't ask me what, for I've no idea — went awry, a couple of hundred years or more back, and the lands, if lands there were, and the money, vanished. The house was sold, the new owners changed the name to 'The Elms', and my people went off to seek their fortunes elsewhere.

'Well, they never did find a fortune, although they did reasonably enough in business. My grandfather started the family firm, my father improved it, and I myself inherited a thriving concern, and built it up yet further by my own efforts. I was still a young man when I determined to retire, more or less, put a manager in charge of the firm, return here and buy the house. And so I did, and changed the name back again.'

'Why that?' I asked, curious.

Mr Emerson laughed. 'I suppose like any exiles, we had fond memories of the ancestral home. After all, my people had lived here for several centuries, so we missed the old place. And there were tales — ' and he broke off, and shrugged.

'Tales?' I said — uncouth, I know, but then I had not been abstemious with regard to the claret, nor was I being abstemious with regard to the brandy.

Mr Emerson did not seem to mind, though. He smiled at me and said tolerantly, 'You know, the usual thing. Tales of a vast fortune hidden about the old place, tales of our being wealthy at one time. True enough, I suppose, as far as it went, for as I say we seem to have had land round about. Certainly we had this house, and you can see for yourselves that it is not the house of a poor man, or it wasn't four or five hundred years ago. Anyway, I certainly never found any pirate treasure under the floorboards, or anything of that sort! But I bought the place out of sentiment, as I say, and then very quickly fell in love with it for itself, and not for any old legends I may have heard at my mother's knee.

'It was four or five years back that we moved here. All seemed set fair, but then two or three years ago things started to go wrong. My wife died; and soon afterwards I myself became ill. I could not keep the business under proper control thanks to my illness, and that foundered; a rascal of a manager put the final touches to it. Then I spent what cash I had in seeking a cure, and it was not until it had pretty well gone that I admitted that no cure was to be found.' He paused, and helped himself to another glass of brandy.

'You have our deepest sympathies, sir,' said Raffles gently, and I stammered my own agreement with this sentiment.

Mr Emerson waved this aside. 'I have

come to terms with my own mortality, at last. Galton, my butler, is also my valet and to some degree my nurse. I realized a short time ago that I could no longer keep a large staff, so when my old butler retired, I looked for a younger man, someone upon whose strength I could depend — and one who would accept a somewhat smaller stipend than the usual, in view of the rapid promotion, as it were!'

'I thought he looked young for a butler,' I muttered.

Mr Emerson nodded. 'So, things move along quite nicely day to day, but as I say, I am concerned now with Letitia's future. That, and this house, for I love the old place, and would like to see it kept in the family, if that could be done.'

Raffles said, 'Presumably a future son-in-law would — '

'He'd need money,' said Mr Emerson shortly. 'Oh, the old place is warm and comfortable enough, but it's gone a bit to pot over the last century. Not been looked after as it should have been. If it's to be decently and sympathetically refurbished — none of this damnable 'restoration', though! — then it will need cash. I had intended to do the job myself, of course, that was to be the task that filled my declining years, my labour of love; but then the money went, as I have just told you. No, anyone who marries Letitia must have plenty of money; and would someone with money want an old barn such as this?' He glanced at us, and laughed. 'Doubtless you think me a mercenary sort of hound? I wouldn't be surprised if you did. But it's all very well being contemptuous about money when you've got it in plenty.'

'Oh, I'm not contemptuous about it!' said Raffles, laughing.

'Nor I!' I added.

Mr Emerson joined in our laughter. 'There is a young chap,' he told us, 'one Gerald Thomas, son of a big landowner in these parts. He'll be here tomorrow, though he's not a member of the Society. I know he's fond of Letitia, and I cultivate him accordingly. If she — that is, if things worked out there, I could be happy enough,' and he swigged his brandy in what I thought a very gloomy fashion.

'And Miss Emerson?' asked Raffles casually.

'Oh, well! A young girl, Mr Raffles, and you know what that means. In an ideal world, if she married 'for love', as they say — well!' He paused, then went on quickly, 'Fact is, she rather prefers another chap, a member of our little Society, chap called Peter Green. But his family, old name and all that, of course, but, well, frankly he hasn't got a bean. So that's out,' and he relapsed into his gloomy mood again.

Soon after this exchange, Raffles excused himself, and I also told our host that it was my bed time. As we reached the head of the stairs, Raffles turned to me, raised an eyebrow and shrugged his shoulders.

'Yes,' said I, taking his meaning, 'it does look like becoming a habit, does it not? 'Advice to the Lovelorn', that sort of thing.'

'Indeed. Well, we now know what it is that troubles our host, Bunny. I must say, you're a good listener, though! Yes, the agony aunt columns of the weekly papers may soon have a new contributor! Or you could try romantic novels; you'd need a false name, of course, 'Bunniella Manders', perhaps?'

'Yes, and my first book would be the story of the Ardagh business!'

He frowned at this, for he hated to be reminded of it, then laughed. 'Touché, Bunny! Well, my boy, whatever Mr Emerson's difficulties, and however much we may sympathize with them, and him, there's nothing we can do in the circumstances. Frankly, I had hoped that we might, that there would be scope for both entertainment and instruction, as it were.' He shrugged. 'As it is — well! I suggest we enjoy the weekend as much as may be possible, then shake the dust of the place off our shoes on Monday, prompt.'

★　★　★

On the following morning, the Saturday, that is to say, I rose early and threw back the curtains to see a blanket of white all around. It was not particularly deep, the snow, but it was certainly seasonable. I shivered, and returned to bed for another hour.

Breakfast was informal, and I was pleased to find that, although both Miss Emerson and Raffles had finished and were nowhere to be seen, our host had risen as late as I myself had. Although he was unable to walk, and could not use his arms without considerable pain, the alertness of his mind had no whit abated, and he spoke on a variety of topics, with poetry chief amongst them. He was, he told me, something of a traditionalist, but admired some of the moderns; and he actually gave high praise to some of my own scribblings! When we had finished, Mr Emerson rather shyly read me some of his own work, heroic blank verse about old battles, Norse heroes, highwaymen and the like. Not my own style, but they seemed to reflect the true man, the man he had been before his illness, is what I mean to say.

It was only natural that I should ask, 'And the other members of your Society? What are their interests, and so forth?'

'I think 'varied' would perhaps be the right word,' said Mr Emerson with a laugh. He glanced up as Galton came in with the morning's post. 'Ah, let's see who we can expect.' He opened a couple of envelopes, and raised an eyebrow. 'As I thought, some of our members have been put off by the weather. But Peter is coming — Peter Green, I mentioned him, he writes verses much in your own style, light-hearted mainly, but with a serious side to them; a bit cynical for my own taste at times, but I suppose that's to be expected under the circumstances, for he hasn't had the good fortune a man has a reasonable right to hope for. Yes. And — ah! Miss Abigail Porter and her sister Miss Emily. Ladies 'of a certain age', as the saying goes; and their verse much as you would expect, kittens and balls of wool, and what have you. Still, they're good people, and they're braving the weather, which is more than you can say for some of our more robust members! D'you know, I think we might have an amusing little gathering, despite the snow.'

'And you mentioned another chap,' I said without thinking, 'a Mr Thomas, was it?'

Mr Emerson's face clouded slightly. 'Gerald Thomas, yes, he'll be here. Mind you, I've — that is, I may have talked out of turn last night, what with the brandy — what with one thing and another. He's certainly fond of Letitia, you can see that at a glance. And his father is — well, let us say Gerald will be able to provide for my daughter, and keep this house up, should things work out, and that's what — that is, it's the main thing.'

I immediately wished I had not spoken, and was looking for a way to change the subject when the doorbell rang. Mr Emerson's face cleared, and he said, 'Ah, that will be the first arrivals. Would you excuse me a moment?' and he turned round the wheeled chair in which he sat, and left the room.

There was a flurry of conversation by the front door, with feminine voices predominant, and then Mr Emerson returned, followed by two ladies whom I took to be Miss Abigail and Miss Emily Porter; and so they proved to be, when Mr Emerson performed the necessary introductions. I took the Misses Porter to be somewhere between forty and fifty; they were both inclined to coquettishness, and to a certain fluttering attitude, but they were likeable and civil — at least at this stage of our acquaintance. There was some bubbling conversation as to the atrocious weather, and the necessity of the sisters staying the night; both had come prepared for that eventuality.

Not long afterwards Mr Peter Green arrived, a man of twenty-two or twenty-three, good looking and articulate enough, if a trifle shy. Hot on his heels came Mr Gerald Thomas, a man of about the same age as Mr Green, but of a very different order; smug and self-satisfied, and a dashed sight more portly than he should have been at that age.

Our reading party being now complete — the others, as Mr Emerson had told me, having cried off on account of the weather — we were all ready, and once hot coffee, chocolate and tea had been offered to the new arrivals as an antidote to the cold, we now got down to some serious business. Raffles pleaded a complete aversion to any poets later than Vergil, and offered to take Miss Emerson, who was similarly indifferent to the muse Calliope, to look at the snow. Mr Thomas rather bristled at this, but he could hardly 'shove his oar in,' as they say, at this late stage, the more so since he had just indicated, in a sneering tone, his intention of sitting in on our proceedings 'to see the fun,' as he rather coarsely put it. He thus had to grin and bear it, or in his case, scowl and bear it, as Raffles and Miss Emerson left, to look in a few moments later, wrapped in furs and so on, before venturing outside.

I have said that Mr Thomas wanted to see the fun; I may add that he certainly got his wish. All literary people are somewhat inclined to what a plain-spoken friend of mine calls 'lady-doggishness,' and of all literary people, poets are by far the worst in this regard. On paper, it may all be 'I wandered lonely as a cloud,' and what have you; but when two or three are gathered together, it is far more likely to be a case of the old stiletto in the back. Oh, discreetly done, of course, you never feel the blade sliding into your ribs: 'Very nice, Mr Manders. Very nice. Yes,' or 'Interesting. But perhaps just a leetle hackneyed, don't you think?' That sort of thing. And I must say that Miss Abigail and Miss Emily were certainly not backward in coming forward with what they described as 'friendly and constructive criticism.'

Mr Thomas, too, made his opinions known, but without any pretence of friendliness or construction, if that is the right word. In short, he was downright rude, managing to reduce poor Miss Emily almost to tears at one stage. But, since I was the guest speaker, it was mostly my own efforts which came in for his special sarcasm. Under different circumstances I might have asked him bluntly to choose between shutting up and clearing out; but I could hardly do that as things were, and Mr Emerson, his mind no doubt on Mr Thomas's fortune, had to content himself with the occasional, 'Now, now, Gerald,' which Thomas simply ignored. I was by no means sorry when we stopped for light refreshments.

Miss Emerson and Raffles returned at about that time, and Thomas immediately rushed to Miss Emerson's side with a sort of offensive proprietorial air, as much as daring Raffles to make something of it! Raffles merely smiled; while I took out my cigar case and suggested that it might be more acceptable to the ladies were I to smoke out in the garden. They fluttered for a time, then agreed, and I dragged Raffles outside with me.

'Well, Bunny,' said he, lighting a Sullivan, 'what do you think to Mr Thomas?'

I told him.

'Yes,' he said with a nod, 'I gather that — allowing for certain differences in phraseology — Miss Emerson shares your views.'

'You surely did not question her about the matter?' said I, shocked.

'Oh, not directly. But it was not too difficult to steer the conversation in that general direction, and then she was positively effusive on the subject. No, it's pretty clearly t'other chap she thinks most of, Mr Green. The trouble, as Mr Emerson said, is money, or the lack thereof.'

'But would she not be happier living in poverty with the man she loves?'

'A poet's outlook, Bunny!' he said with a smile that was almost a sneer. 'But, no, for Miss Emerson has taken to heart her father's wish that the house should be kept in the family, and Mr Green's resources would not even cover the day-to-day running of the place, let alone any improvements, repairs and renovations. If this Green chap had money, of course, or the Emersons had, it might be different,' he mused, half to himself. He thought for a moment, then shook himself, partly to remove the flakes of snow that had settled on his coat, and partly, as it seemed to me, to dismiss the matter from his mind. 'Still, bricks without clay! If I had any spare cash, of course, I'd part with it like a shot in the interests of true love. As it is . . . ' Another shrug completed the sentence; and I confessed that my own sentiments were much the same. All the sympathy in the world was available for the asking for Mr and Miss Emerson, and the luckless Mr Green; but practical financial help was another matter altogether.

When we resumed our studies, I had a somewhat easier time of it, for now it was the turn of the others to read their work, my own task being to comment upon it. I can claim no special expertise as a critic, but at least I had been published — though seldom paid! — and that bestowed a cachet on my work and my opinions. I tried to be as kind as possible, and in fact their verses were not too bad, provided always that you overlooked a tendency on the part of the Misses Porter to sentimentalize about cats and small children. So we got on rather well, with the only corpulent fly in the ointment being Mr Thomas, who steered Miss Emerson — very much against her will — into a corner of the room, and kept muttering what were evidently intended to be humorous remarks about our deliberations, punctuated by guffaws of coarse laughter, into her ear. Of Raffles there was no sign, and I assumed that he had merely decided to avoid the unpleasant Mr Thomas, a decision with which I could sympathize.

By the time we broke up for luncheon, I had pretty well had enough of Mr Thomas to last me a lifetime, and when he repeated the morning's performance in the afternoon, the sole difference being that his comments were now louder and more offensive, I determined to do something about it. Had Raffles been there to keep me in countenance, things might have been different, but he had muttered something about going into the village for some tobacco, then vanished from sight.

That determination became a definite resolve at dinner. Partly this was because I again indulged rather freely in Mr Emerson's wine — understandable, given the provocations of the day, I'm sure you will agree! But partly, too, it was due to Thomas's behaviour. He behaved as if he had bought and paid for the house, Miss

Emerson, Mr Emerson, and the rest of us for good measure. His talk was all of money, and how marvellous it was to have it. He wore a gold watch with a chain like the anchor cable of a Transatlantic liner, and he pulled that out and told us how much it had cost; and he was similarly communicative with regard to his rings, his cigarette case, and his dress studs.

As I have said, I had drunk freely of our host's wine, but I knew as much; and I knew that I must be sober later that night. Accordingly I refused any liqueurs, asking instead for a black coffee, pleading a slight headache. The same excuse served to explain my going to bed before the others, and as I left the room, Raffles followed me.

'Are you quite all right, Bunny?'

'Oh, yes, thanks, Raffles. Just had enough of that fellow in there, that's all.'

'Yes, he is a beauty, isn't he? Still — ' and he shrugged. 'I rather wanted a word, my boy, but as you're obviously feeling rather seedy, it had better wait until tomorrow,' and he bade me good night.

I left him, and went to my room. I kept my evening trousers on, they were dark enough, but changed my white shirt for a black jersey. Then I lay down to rest, and to clear my head. I am ashamed to admit that I actually dozed off, and only by chance did I wake in time to carry out my plans. Still, wake I did, and a glance at my watch showed that it was almost two o'clock. Thomas should be sound asleep by now, for he had been imbibing even more freely than I had at dinner, and besides he had not refused brandy, as I had, afterwards.

Accordingly, I let myself out, and crept down the corridor. My room was on the first floor, and so was that of Thomas, but his was the other side of the landing. Now, there was a large window on the landing, and this window was directly over the front door; the front door had a little porch, and the porch was covered with an ancient, gnarled ivy plant. It will be obvious, then, that even an unathletic man would have little difficulty gaining access to the landing window. I opened the window, and made a few scratches round the catch with the blade of my penknife, then I pulled the window to, but left the catch open. That, I hoped, would suggest to the police that some burglar had shinned up the ivy of the porch and jemmied the window open.

The window dealt with, I continued across the landing and down the corridor, hoping that Thomas was not so doubting of his fellow guests as to lock his bedroom door. I need not have worried. It opened silently, and I glided inside. The curtains were not properly closed, and the moonlight reflected from the snow outside showed me the various items of furniture quite clearly. I made my way to the side of the bed.

Now, it will be obvious that my intention was to rob the odious Thomas. I would take his watch and chain, his dress studs and cufflinks, his rings if he took them off to sleep, and such cash as he might have upon his person. I should conceal the booty whilst the police investigated the 'jemmied' window and reached the incorrect conclusion; I should sell the booty on returning to London;

then I should fake a letter from a fictitious firm of legal men to Mr Green, saying that his old Uncle Herbert had just died in Australia or somewhere, and enclosing a cheque, ostensibly a bequest under Uncle Herbert's will, and in reality the proceeds of the sale of the loot.

Reader, I know what you are thinking! 'A drop in the ocean,' perhaps, or 'Not worth the candle.' Something on those lines. In short, however highly priced a watch or cufflinks or the rest might be to the legitimate purchaser, the amount they would raise from a 'fence' would not keep Mr Green in cigars for more than a week! True, all true; but then it was mostly that I wanted to get back at Thomas, to take from him that which was his; not for myself, but to provide something — anything — to Mr Green. It was, in a word, the principle of the thing.

None of which actually mattered, because as I reached the bed, I saw that the sheets were undisturbed. Not only was Thomas not in bed, he had not yet been to bed!

I stood there, cold sober by now, but

still befuddled. Where the devil was the fellow? My first horrid thought — and my blood ran cold — was that he was forcing his unwelcome attentions on Miss Emerson. But no! I dismissed that at once. More probably he had collapsed over the brandy, and the others had left him there to sleep it off! Again, no; I would have left him, Raffles would have left him, Green would probably have left him, but Mr Emerson would never play so inhospitable a trick. The only reasonable explanation was that Thomas was still downstairs guzzling Mr Emerson's cognac! At two o'clock in the morning? Well, what other —

A footfall on the landing put an end to further speculation. Yes, clearly he had been swilling his drink, equally clearly he was now sated, very clearly he was now staggering towards the welcoming arms of Morpheus!

I shot a hasty glance around the room. The opportunities for concealment were limited in the extreme. In fact, there was only one possible hiding place, a cupboard of sorts built into the wall opposite the door. In less time than it takes to write, I had the door open, and thrust myself inside.

The cupboard — if that is the right word — was tall enough to hold a man, as it went from floor to ceiling. But it was tiny, smaller than any artisan's pantry. Too small, in fact, to be of any use for anything but a wardrobe; and as I encountered Thomas's suits and trousers hanging in there, I recollected that I had exactly the same sort of cupboard built in to the wall of my own room,and that, in the absence of what I might call a freestanding wardrobe, it was arranged, and I had used it, for precisely the same purpose.

Now, the difficulty was that Thomas was wearing evening dress, and he would very naturally want to disrobe before he went to bed! It was, of course, perfectly possible that he would leave his things on a chair, or indeed on the floor; he certainly struck me as the sort of man who would be careless of his clothes, and then berate his unfortunate valet because of their crumpled state. But suppose he did not? As that thought crossed my mind, and as the bedroom door opened, I pushed myself as far to the back of the clothes as I could.

And the side of the cupboard gave way! I mean that quite literally — the wall, or what had seemed to be the wall, moved inwards before me, and I half stepped, half fell, into a space that was the image of the wardrobe itself, save for the fact that this was empty.

'A secret passage?' I hear you ask. And I hear the disappointment in your voice.

Well, it was not a passage, or not as far as I could tell. But it was a secret room — or at least a concealed room. Not so surprising, when you think about it, for the house was five centuries old, and we have all heard of Priest's Holes, and the like. In any event, I all but fell into the thing, and the door closed behind me, leaving me in total darkness.

There was a sound in the bedroom, and a flash of light fell upon my startled eyes. For a horrid moment I really thought that I had been discovered. But then I realized that there was a spy hole of sorts in one wall of my hiding place. I put an eye to it, and had a view, limited to be sure, of the bedroom beyond. I made out Thomas, lighting a second lamp, and staring, as it seemed to my anxious eye, directly at me. 'What was that?' he asked, his voice low, presumably so as not to wake the whole house.

'Oh,' said a second voice, 'rats in the wainscotting! An old place like this, only to be expected.' I recognized the voice — Galton, the butler. But speaking with a familiarity that was very different from the tone expected from a man in his position. And anyway, what was Galton still doing up at two o'clock and later? Unless he were escorting the befuddled Thomas, and spoke thus lightly knowing that the other man would have no recollection next day of what had happened?

Apparently not, though, for Thomas said, 'Rats be damned! I'm having a look in that wardrobe!' And he marched towards the door with the stride of a sober, and a determined, man.

I shrank back yet further, half hoping that there might be yet a third chamber!

There was not, but Thomas was evidently unaware of the concealed room in which I cowered, for he rummaged in the wardrobe section next to me for a moment, then turned away with a grunt. 'You must be right,' he told Galton. 'This place probably does have rats. I'll be glad to get rid of it.'

'Ah, but don't be too hasty! We must find it first.'

'Yes. And you have no clue?'

Galton was now in my field of view, and I saw him shake his head. 'No idea. Not even the least notion of what — 'it' — might be. Talk, of course, but vague talk, and that's all. Have you found out anything?'

'Not a - - - thing!' said Thomas, disgruntled.

'Well, then,' said Galton, in a very significant tone — though what the tone signified, I could not begin to imagine.

Thomas gave a snort indicative of disapproval or perhaps of anger. 'You've been here three months,' he said petulantly.

'I know. But it isn't as easy as you

might think, for the old man never leaves the house, and then I must be alert for the bell whenever he rings it. Besides, a rambling old place like this, it would take a dozen men years to search it properly.'

'H'mm.' Thomas sounded slightly, though not completely, mollified.

'So,' Galton continued, 'you'll just have to play the man. It isn't too bad, after all, the girl isn't bad looking.'

It was not merely his familiar tone which shocked and disgusted me, but the words themselves. 'The girl' could only be Miss Emerson, and here was her father's butler speaking about her as if she were — well, a scullery maid, if not worse!

Thomas was mumbling something like, 'All very well for you ... Attractive enough, but it's the money ... Great old place like this ... ' and he ended by cursing roundly in a louder voice than he had used up until then.

Galton shushed him to silence, then said, 'We had better continue our deliberations tomorrow.' He went to the door, made a mock bow, and asked in a sardonic tone, 'If there is nothing more, sir?'

Thomas indicated coarsely that there was not. Galton left, closing the door softly behind him. Thomas, left alone, swore again, his anger distinctly directed against Galton this time, not for any specific reason that I could make out, but rather in the nature of a man who had been bottling up his emotions and vents his anger on the nearest available object, however unreasonable the process may be. When he had pretty well exhausted his vocabulary — after having enlarged mine quite considerably — he turned off the gas, leaving only a candle by the bed for illumination, and began to undress. I averted my eyes, and when I looked again the room was in darkness.

I think you will allow that my position was an unenviable one. I had entered the bedroom assuming that Thomas was abed and asleep. Had he woken I should have silenced him with a blow, or thrown the sheets over him, or something of that kind; in a word, I was prepared to do violence in the course of my robbery, to avoid being caught. But this hole and corner business — in the most literal sense — was entirely different.

I did not know whether I would be better staying there all night, and leaving in the morning, when Thomas went down to breakfast; at first I thought this might be best, but then I got to thinking what would happen if the maid went into my own room, to find it empty. Nothing too odd about that, but then if I were missed, and the maid spoke up, there would be some awkward questions. I could always plead that I had gone out to walk in the snow, gain inspiration for my next poem, of course, but there was still a considerable element of danger in waiting for daylight; too many folk around, to put it shortly.

On balance, my best bet was to move in the dark, clear out and seek the sanctuary of my own room. I have said that Thomas had been swigging wine and brandy at the dinner table; I did not know if he had kept up the same pace whilst I had been dozing on my bed, but even if he had not, he had still taken a good deal more on board than most men would have found necessary. With that, and the lateness of the hour, it should not take too long for him to fall asleep, and then I would go.

While I waited for Thomas to nod off, I did some hard thinking. It was obvious that Thomas and Galton were confederates, that they had some nefarious scheme in hand. But what? Whether Galton had taken the lowly paid job only to gain access to the house, or whether Thomas had recognized a fellow rogue and suborned the butler, the result was the same. Galton, on his own admission, had been searching the house for 'it' — for something or the other, without success. But, again — what? What was he looking for? And then why was Thomas acting as if he were unwilling to marry Miss Emerson? I knew of, and could understand, her reluctance to marry him, but why should he cavil at the match? And then — although I had only caught snatches of their talk, for as I say they had kept their voices low — but it sounded very much as if 'money' had been mentioned; the sense of it, as I had followed it, being that Thomas hoped to gain financially by marrying Miss Emerson, when exactly the reverse had previously seemed the case!

I gave it up. I would talk the matter over with Raffles later, see if he had any ideas. Meantime, Thomas was snoring loudly, and it was time for me to go.

A further problem now obtruded on my tired brain. I could not find the catch or spring that opened the hidden door! I ran my hand over the side of the room through which I had entered, but without success. Increasingly desperate, I explored the entire inner surface of the place. I thought I had found it as my hands reached the top corner of the walls opposite the entrance, but it was merely a disgusting mass of spiders' webs and dust — no! There was something else there, tucked into a sort of shelf high up, something that felt like a wedge of papers. It was, of course, pitch black in there, and I could make no sort of examination of my find; all I could do was stuff the package, for such it seemed to be, under my jersey.

I ran my hands round the walls again, more urgently this time, and by some miracle I must have touched the secret spring, or whatever moved the wall, for the side of the room slid back and I tumbled through into the wardrobe proper.

I pulled the hidden door and it slid back and clicked shut. As quietly as I could, I opened the wardrobe door and went into the bedroom. Thomas, as I say, was snoring away, and by the light the filtered through the half closed curtains I could make out his watch and jewellery on the bedside table.

Well, I had intended to rob him, and I might as well make a decent job of that, at any rate! In a moment I had taken his jewellery and notecase from the table and pocketed them.

And then, with a blessed sense of relief, I was out in the corridor, and headed for safety! I crossed the landing, noting with satisfaction that the window was just a touch ajar, and set off down the opposite corridor.

I had got halfway along when there was

a slight sound to my right. I turned my head, but before I could properly see what might be happening, someone had an arm round my chest, while another went round my neck and a hand was clamped over my mouth! I was dragged bodily along for a couple of yards, then flung down with considerable violence.

I turned hastily, and saw — Raffles!

'Raffles!'

'You, Bunny?' He laughed silently, and handed me his cigarette case.

I sat up and looked round. I was in Raffles' room, and he had flung me down upon his bed.

'I was sure you were a burglar!' he told me. 'I heard you creep along the corridor hours ago — '

'Surely not?'

'Well, you would have fooled almost anyone else, but not me, Bunny! Anyway, I took a look, but there was nobody about. I did notice that the window appeared to have been tampered with, and that confirmed my suspicions.' He laughed again. 'I must say, Bunny, it was an odd sensation! Being in a house that was being burgled by someone else, I mean. Well, I waited, and when I heard you creeping back, I assumed that you — the burglar, that is — had cleaned out the rooms on the far side of the landing, and planned to do the same this side. So, I waited by the door, and you know the rest.' He regarded me curiously. 'I must say, you look as if you've had some rare adventures, Bunny! Your clothes are filthy. Are those your dress trousers? It would break your tailor's heart.'

'Raffles, I've overheard a most intriguing conversation. In Thomas's room.'

'What?'

'Yes, I went there to rob him, you know — '

'What?'

'Oh, I had some idea of taking his jewellery and things, and sending the proceeds to young Green, to help him out, you know.'

'I trust you did not put this 'idea' into practice?'

It was my turn to surprise Raffles! 'Oh, yes.' Proudly, I produced my spoils.

'You young idiot!'

'Raffles?'

He pulled his curtains aside, and waved a hand. I stood up, puzzled, and looked out at a fine blanket of snow.

'So much for your jemmied window,' said Raffles sarcastically. 'You will observe that the weather conditions have made it perfect for the creation, retention and exhibition of tracks to and from the house.'

'Well? Oh!' I sat down, the full horror of my actions beginning to dawn upon me. 'You mean there won't be any tracks to and from the house?'

'Just so.'

'It will be obvious that the robber is someone in the house.'

'Indeed.'

I thought a moment. 'Raffles, I don't suppose I could go outside — '

'No,' he said shortly. 'The only thing to be done is to return those bits and pieces. And immediately at that.'

I stood up. 'Very well.'

He waved me to sit down. 'I shall go,' he said, gathering up my armful of trophies. 'You stay here.' And before I could say anything, he had turned down the gas and slipped out into the corridor, closing the door after him.

I sat there for what seemed like an age, though it can have been no more than two or three minutes. Then the door opened, and Raffles came back into the room. 'Now, Bunny,' he said, 'You mentioned an interesting conversation, I think?'

I told him what had occurred, and what I had overheard pass between Thomas and Galton.

He listened in silence, then said, 'You were hidden in his wardrobe, you say?'

'No, Raffles, in a sort of Priest's Hole thing at the back of it!'

'So, there's one in there as well, is there?'

'Raffles?'

'Well, Bunny, it's a murky business, but one could hazard a guess at what these villains have in mind, could one not?'

'Could one, Raffles?'

'Ah, I was forgetting. You recollect that I mentioned after dinner that I had some news to impart, Bunny? When I went into the village this afternoon, I made some discreet enquiries at the local inn. You will know that Mr Thomas, or his father, I should say, is the biggest landowner round these parts? Well, there is apparently some hint of irregularity about the claim the Thomas family has to the lands. There is a local tale, a legend almost, to the effect that the Emerson family was somehow cheated by the Thomas family out of their fortune. Some say it was in the Civil War, some that it was more recently. In any event, one of the tenants on the lands owned by Mr Thomas has challenged Thomas to produce the original deeds, land grants and so on, but so far he has failed to do so. The same tenant, a retired army man of pronounced views, is rumoured to be taking legal advice.'

I stared at him for a moment, then, 'Raffles? I wonder — ' and I produced my bundle of dusty papers from beneath my even dustier jersey.

★   ★   ★

I slept badly that night, or that morning, I should say. Raffles had glanced at the papers I had found, then, laughing in an unholy fashion, he had bundled me out of his room and told me that he would arrange matters, and I was merely to follow his lead. 'But you really did very well, Bunny,' he told me as he left me at my door. 'Yes, very well indeed!'

On Raffles' orders, I waited until he tapped on my door the next morning, and we went down to breakfast together.

The others were all assembled there, and we nodded a greeting as we entered the room. Raffles sauntered over to the sideboard, and as helped himself he glanced at Mr Emerson. 'You know, sir, I'm really here under what one might call false pretences,' he said.

'Oh? And why do you say that, Mr Raffles?'

'I have visited your lovely house before, that's all I meant. Of course, it was called 'The Elms' then. An interesting place, like all these old houses. You know about the Priest's Hole, of course?' he added casually, as he moved to the table.

Thomas was seated opposite me, and he sat up and took notice at that, I can tell you!

'Priest's Hole?' asked Mr Emerson. He shook his head. 'No, I never heard of such a thing.'

'Oh, but there is one,' said Raffles. 'In this room, as a matter of fact.'

Naturally there was a hubbub of questions and comments at this, and Raffles was urged to reveal the secret chamber.

He smiled as he ate his breakfast, and when he had done, he said, 'Shall I demonstrate the hidden door?'

'Oh, you must!' cried everyone together.

'Well, then.' Raffles got up and strolled over to the massive chimney. He ran his hand over the inside surface. 'Somewhere here, I think — ah!'

There was a gentle click, and one of the great oak timbers that stood at the sides of the chimney swung inwards.

'What's it like?' and 'What's in there?' came from the spectators.

Raffles shrugged his shoulders. 'It was shown to us when last I was here,' he said, 'but none of us ever went into it. It looks very dusty, and I'm sure there must be dozens of spiders in there.'

'Oh, spiders!' cried Miss Abigail and Miss Emily.

Raffles glanced round the room. 'I suppose in the interests of historical research — here, Bunny, your clothes are the shabbiest of anyone's, why don't you do the honours?'

'Indeed, Raffles!' I moved quickly, before Thomas or anyone else could take the initiative. 'Beastly dark in here,' I complained as I went in and pulled the door to. 'Dusty, as you said.'

'Nothing interesting in there, is there, Bunny?' asked Raffles in the most casual tone imaginable. 'Only one does always rather think of hidden treasure, and what have you.'

'Nothing, Raffles.' I was about to leave, disappointed, and then — having, after all, some expertise in this sort of thing by now! — I bethought me of the shelf I had found in the other secret room, and ran my hands round the walls. 'Oh!'

'Bunny?'

I emerged slowly from the chamber, the bundle of papers — placed there by Raffles, of course, as I now realized — in my hands. I laid them on the table before Mr Emerson. 'Can't quite make them out, sir,' I said, 'but they look rather like deeds to me.'

8

THE OTHER SIDE

I have remarked elsewhere, and in passing, that my friend AJ Raffles had a considerable experience of the fair sex. I have deliberately avoided any more circumstantial discussion of this topic, for what I trust are obvious reasons. However, the trial and conviction of the man who now calls himself 'Sebastian Melmoth' produced what I can only describe as a mood of suspicion or innuendo, a kind of schoolboy sniggering whenever two men were seen dining together. So perhaps it is not entirely inappropriate to include here a story which sheds a little light upon this aspect of Raffles' character; you will, I know, understand that it is still necessary for me to be imprecise, if not downright untruthful, as to some of the details.

It was autumn, in a year which I shall

not name but which was not very far from the second Jubilee of Queen Victoria. I had seen nothing much of Raffles since the cricket season faded out, he seemed to have vanished from view. As for me, my own modest literary efforts were at last meeting with a certain amount of financial success. So much so, indeed, that editors were now contacting me, rather than the other way round! Not exactly in droves, you understand, and the money, when it came, was not in such quantity as I might have wished for; but it was what I might call optimistic rather than the reverse, it all meant that I was considerably cheered by the way things were going. And since I was now earning some cash legitimately, it meant, too, that I had no incentive to seek out Raffles with the purpose of joining in some dangerous and criminal scheme to make money.

On the day of which I am writing I had received a cheque far more munificent than the usual meagre specimens of its kind to which I had perforce become accustomed. The day was one of those bright and sunny exceptions to the dullness of the season that sometimes help to hasten October's passing, and I spent it wandering round the shops and replenishing my wardrobe, which had become somewhat run-down of late. It ought to have been a perfect day; but yet as I strolled from tailor's to shirtmaker's, I experienced a curious, almost an oppressive, sensation, rather as if I were being watched. I could not explain it, other than to think that my sudden good fortune had perhaps led to a touch of that hubris which so bothered the ancient Greeks, and that this was the reaction to that. I shook off the feeling with a stiff drink at the Criterion bar, and thoroughly enjoyed the afternoon.

I determined to round the day off with a respectable dinner, and at around half past eight I went along to my favourite restaurant — to find it closed for refurbishment! I had not known of the proposed redecoration, for insufficiency of funds had meant I had not patronized the place for some time. I ought, of course, to have gone there in the afternoon, and would then have had sufficient time to think about a reservation elsewhere; but one does not always think of these things. It was not exactly the end of the world, to be sure, but I muttered to myself that it rather took the gilt off the gingerbread.

Then thoughts of that humble food-stuff jogged my memory. Some days before, a friend of mine had recommended a small place, 'The Carlton Workmen's Eating Rooms,' on the fringes of the East End, not so far east that one would appear to be 'slumming,' but out of the usual run of high-class restaurants. Their pie and mash, jellied eels, and the like, said my friend, would put many a West End hotel to shame. He and a few friends had discovered the place in the early hours some time before, and they were keeping it very much to themselves, lest the bright young things should learn of it and spoil it.

Well, I had eaten much more spartan fare than pie and mash, thought I (and, did I but know it then, I would eat even less well a year or two later, when I served my eighteen months in Wormwood

Scrubs!) so why should I not try the place, which was, after all, at no great distance away? I should be fed, and at less cost than I had originally planned for, thereby producing a feeling of virtue that would counter to some extent my spendthrift behaviour of the afternoon. Moreover, the other customers would surely be worth the attention of a literary man, and would doubtless provide material for a few paragraphs illustrative of life in the East End. The way my luck was running at the moment, there would be no difficulty about selling such character sketches to one of the weekly papers!

Almost imagining myself a new Dickens or Mayhew, I set off at a brisk walk — no cabs for me tonight! In a very short while I had left the fashionable West End proper, and found myself in a somewhat dreary and all but deserted street. This was not yet the true East End, but that no man's land of not-quite-poor but yet shabby houses that are home alike to the artisan moving up in the world, and the aristocrat going down.

I had gone halfway along the street

when a hubbub of voices caught my attention. The sound was not in any sense that of a dispute or altercation, more the noise you get when a crowd leaves a theatre after a show. I glanced ahead of me, and saw a throng of people emerging from a large, brick building that I had all but reached. The legend 'Mission Hall,' or some such, was over the door, and as I neared the place I could see a poster, 'Spiritualist Meeting — Tonight!' plastered on the wall by the door.

Feeling that neither the building, nor the meeting, nor, to be blunt, the people, would hold any great appeal for me, I moved aside to avoid the crowd spilling on to the pavement. Then I spotted a familiar figure, none other than that of AJ Raffles, and by his side a most attractive young woman. Ahah! thought I, so that is why his friends have seen little of old Raffles of late! Mind you, I could not blame him in the least, for the young woman was dark, well dressed, and quite lovely to look at.

'Hullo!' I said as I passed them — I did not use Raffles' name, for you were never absolutely sure with him that he was going about under his true identity.

He looked guilty; not the guilt of a man engaged upon some criminal enterprise, but the guilt of a man caught with an attractive young woman of whose existence his friends have hitherto been ignorant. 'Hullo, Bunny! Ah — Mr Manders, Miss Ellison.'

I mumbled the usual pleasantries, but then felt at something of a loss. I could hardly invite someone like Miss Ellison, who was clearly well-bred, to share pie and mash with Raffles and myself! And besides, I did not know if she and Raffles might have plans for the rest of the evening. So I ended by saying, 'I fear I must go — an engagement,' or something of that kind.

Raffles nodded. 'We have not talked for some time, Bunny,' he told me. 'Call on me in my rooms at noon tomorrow, if you like.' I promised that I would do so, and started off again, only to halt a second time when I saw the angular form of Inspector Mackenzie, of Scotland Yard, emerge from the doorway! He had the furtive air of a man who does not want to be seen; and it seemed very much to me as if he were following Raffles.

I stood there for a long moment, wondering just what the devil might be going on. By the time I had decided that the best course would be to march boldly up to Mackenzie and greet him openly, force the issue, he was almost at the end of the street, while of Raffles and the young lady there was no sign. I gave it up for the moment and went on my way, determined to question Raffles thoroughly on the morrow.

I had my pie and mash. The friend who had recommended the place had been right, it was food fit for the gods, though I fear that I hardly did it justice; and I had no inclination to observe my fellow diners for those lively paragraphs of which I had dreamed earlier. My mind was in a whirl, but to no good effect, for neither in the eating rooms, nor on the walk back to Mount Street, nor in the hours that preceded my dropping off to sleep, could I imagine what Raffles was up to, or Mackenzie either for that matter.

Was Raffles planning to rob Miss Ellison, or some member of her family? I could not think so, for his attitude had been that of a squire rather than a knave. Then why was Mackenzie following Raffles and Miss Ellison? For I could think of no other reason why Mackenzie should be in that run-down neighbourhood just at the precise time that Raffles and his lady friend happened to be there. And above all, why was Raffles, the most prosaic, if not the most cynical, of men, attending a Spiritualist meeting?

I invented several theories, each more bizarre than the last, and discarded them each in turn, before giving the matter up and going to sleep.

★ ★ ★

At noon the next day, I rang Raffles' bell in the Albany, and he let me in. 'Hullo, Bunny!'

I regarded him with some suspicion. 'Don't tell me you've become a Spiritualist, Raffles?'

'Good Lord — '

'And what was Mackenzie doing there?'

He gave a slight start, then his face cleared and he laughed. 'Was Mr Mac there? I didn't see him, Bunny. Mind you, I can't tell yet whether it's a good thing or a bad.'

I leaned forward. 'Raffles, I haven't seen anything of you for absolutely ages. When I do run into you — quite by chance — you are escorting a very attractive young woman, you have been to a Spiritualist meeting, and you are being shadowed by Detective Inspector Mackenzie of Scotland Yard! I think you owe me a drink, Raffles, and a cigar, Raffles, and above all things an explanation, Raffles!'

He got to his feet. 'Here's the drink, Bunny, and there are the cigars on the table.'

'And the explanations?'

Raffles sat down again, lit a Sullivan, and gave what in any other man I should call a sheepish laugh. Then he told me the following tale.

He had, it seems, met Miss Ellison quite by chance. He was vague as to the

exact circumstances, and I rather suspected that he had been surveying some
house with what you would call a
professional eye; that Miss Ellison was
one of the inhabitants of said house; and
that, on meeting her, he had altered his
plans slightly. This suspicion, unworthy
though it might be, grew stronger when
he added that Miss Ellison lived with, and
acted as a sort of companion to, her aunt,
who was also called Miss Ellison. (For the
sake of clarity, I shall try to refer to the
younger Miss Ellison as 'Miss Dora,' that
being her name -spoken by Raffles in a
sort of faraway tone, a tone that sent a
cold shiver down my spine — and the
aunt I shall call 'Miss Ellison.')

Now, the aunt, Miss Ellison, was a keen
Spiritualist, and Miss Dora had been
obliged to accompany the older lady to
several seances, and had developed what
you might call a sort of academic interest
in the subject, though according to
Raffles she was by no means as convinced
as her aunt as to the honesty of the various practitioners. When Raffles appeared
on the scene, he too was expected to

escort the Misses Ellison to various sittings.

'Good Lord!' said I at this juncture. 'But you don't tell me that you've taken any sort of interest in the subject yourself?'

He regarded me severely. 'Only in a strictly businesslike sense, Bunny. You would be surprised just how many people take the subject seriously. Men who have reached the top of their various professions, serious-minded scientists. Oh, not all of them believe the claims of the 'mediums', of course, in fact some of those sceptics who aim to discredit the subject show the keenest interest in it, for fairly obvious reasons. No, I have seen nothing that might make me a believer; but I have observed that the seances fall into two distinct classes. You have the sort of general meeting that you saw me visit last night, that is open to all comers, and the content of which is usually pretty vague, a sort of introduction to the benefits of belief, lantern slides showing 'apparitions' or 'apports', or whatever the right word may be, that sort of thing.

Then you have more intense, more serious sittings, a few earnest individuals meeting in a private house, asking specific questions, or hoping for specific messages from the other side. It is mainly the latter that interest Miss Ellison's aunt, and which interest me.'

'But it was one of the 'open to all' things you were at last night,' I pointed out, 'and I did not see the elder Miss Ellison with you then.'

He held up a hand. 'Bear with me, Bunny. I have said that my interest was strictly professional, and you know what that means. In a word, it struck me that if a man knew who would be at seance on a certain evening, shall we say — '

'He would know that their houses would be empty, or at least emptier?'

'You read my mind, Bunny. And of course, although a lot of people are interested in the subject in a vague kind of way, in that they will go along to a free meeting like last night's, the number of those in central London who take it seriously enough to hold a seance in their own homes, pay a medium such as

Madame Carati — '

'Who?'

'Madame Carati. Famous medium, though you won't have heard of her. She was at the meeting last night. But don't keep interrupting a fellow, Bunny! I was saying that there aren't that many people here in town who take it seriously; and hence they are fairly easy to keep track of. And most of them are rich, or getting on that way. Well, I had pretty well made up my mind that I should have a shot at the thing, when someone or the other beat me to it!'

I frowned. 'In what way?'

'Listen. I was at a seance, at Miss Ellison's house, as a matter of fact, and was listening pretty keenly to the conversation before the main event, to learn who would be at the next seance, with a view to selecting my victim. Madame Carati went through her performance — and pretty mediocre it was, too, Bunny — and I stayed to a little supper. Imagine how I felt the next day when I learned that old Colonel Browne, who had been seated next to me at the seance, had been robbed! And just during the exact time we had been at Miss Ellison's.'

'Great minds think alike, eh, Raffles?'

He nodded. 'Evidently. And then the same thing happened on the evening of the next seance, too. I was not present at that seance, and nor was I 'working'. But I had studied the list of those who might be there, and selected two of them as being likely candidates. It was one of my two names who was robbed.'

'So, someone who thinks on very similar lines to you, then?'

Another nod. 'And then Inspector Mackenzie drifted on to the scene! The devil of it was, with my having been seen at some of the seances, he suspected me at once. Of course, as it was, I had nothing to hide — genuinely had nothing to hide, for once! — so I wasn't too worried. Mackenzie was a bit thrown by the fact that I was actually present at a seance when the first robbery took place, but I'm sure he thought that I had somehow worked the trick there! He's been following me ever since — '

'Me, too!' I exclaimed, for I had just

seen the explanation for the curious sensation of being followed that I had felt the day before. I gave Raffles a quick account of my own experiences.

Raffles nodded sagely. 'I have no doubt you are right, Bunny,' he said, frowning. 'What with your being what Mackenzie would call 'a known associate' of mine, he would wish to be informed of your doings.' He rubbed his chin thoughtfully. 'Yes. He most likely suspects that I was at the seance that first time to provide myself with an alibi, whilst you were doing the robbery!'

'I say!'

'And then of course he himself must have followed me to the meeting last night, though I confess I did not spot him. He must be improving!'

'But this is intolerable, Raffles!' I burst out.

'I heartily agree, Bunny. It leaves a chap no chance at all to get on with his work!'

I emitted a snort of disgust. 'I have been legitimately employed these last few weeks, Raffles, with no thought of anything untoward in my mind. Why should I be subjected to this persecution, merely because — ' and just in time I realized what I was saying, and stopped.

'Merely because you happen to be a friend of mine, Bunny?'

'That isn't what I meant, Raffles, and well you know it! But suppose I had to meet some editor or publisher, and half Scotland Yard came trailing after me, how would that look? And all because — merely because — of some unproven suspicion on Mackenzie's part!'

He gazed at me in silence for a long moment, then nodded thoughtfully. 'I agree, something must be done about it, and soon.' He rang the bell for the doorman, then took out a silver propelling pencil that had once graced the window of a jeweller's in Bond Street, found some paper, and scribbled a note. When the doorman arrived, Raffles handed him the note and a couple of shillings, and said, 'Would you get a messenger boy to take that round to Inspector Mackenzie at Scotland Yard?'

I fairly gasped at this, and the doorman had gone by the time I had recovered sufficiently to stammer out, 'Raffles! What are you thinking of?'

'The only sensible course of action, Bunny, I assure you. As long as this other fellow is at liberty and at work, Mackenzie will stick so close to us that we shall be quite unable to — well, to do anything that we might wish.'

'But, Raffles! To assist Mackenzie?'

He shrugged. 'Some of our exploits have been a touch equivocal, Bunny. The penalty we pay for not being professionals, of course.'

'Even so, Raffles!' said I, so taken aback by this going over to what in the circumstances it seemed appropriate to think of as 'the other side' that I did not think to query his use of 'we,' or 'us,' or 'our.'

He waved me to silence with an impatient gesture, then lit a cigarette. After five minutes, I ventured to ask, 'Why exactly were you at the public meeting last night? You never told me that.'

'Ah.' He looked embarrassed at this and would have changed the subject if he dared, but I was in no mood to let him off the hook. 'Two reasons, Bunny. The first being that I had a suspicion that Madame Carati herself might be involved, or her accomplice, I should say.'

'What, the old dear spies out the land, passes information on to the actual burglar?'

He nodded. 'Something of that sort. But I hardly think that is likely. No,' he added almost to himself, 'it's a one-man show if ever I saw one.'

'And the other reason for your going there? You said there were two.'

'Indeed.' He coughed delicately. 'The fact is, Dora — Miss Ellison the younger, that is to say — rather wanted to go and see the fun.'

'Ah.' I had more questions, of course, but he gave that dismissive wave of the hand a second time, and sat there smoking his Sullivans in silence until there was a tap at the door, and the lean form of Inspector Mackenzie insinuated itself into the room.

Mackenzie nodded a greeting, and regarded me suspiciously before asking, 'I had word you wished to see me, Mr Raffles?'

'I did indeed, Inspector Mackenzie. Won't you hang up your hat and coat and take a seat? Perhaps a whisky? Or a cigar?'

'I won't drink on duty, thank you — and besides, it's a trifle early in the day for me,' said Mackenzie. 'But I'll not refuse a cigar, thank you kindly. Now,' he went on when once his figurado was alight, 'what was it you wanted, sir?'

Raffles leaned forward in his chair, and studied his old adversary intently. 'It's about these robberies that have been taking place during Spiritualist seances,' he said quietly.

Mackenzie dropped his cigar, and scrambled to retrieve it from the carpet. 'No harm done. Sorry, Mr Raffles, you were saying . . . ?'

'I was saying that I have a theory about these robberies which have taken place whilst honest — albeit rather gullible — folk are attending Spiritualist meetings. I take it that you are handling the case, for Scotland Yard would naturally want their best man on it?'

Mackenzie strove manfully to look modest. 'Aye, well it's maybe not for me to say as much, Mr Raffles. However, you're right in thinking that I have been put in charge of the matter. You have a theory, you say? Well, I'd be most interested to hear it, for I have some notions of my own, you know.'

'To be sure, Mr Mac, and I wouldn't dream of setting up my ideas against yours, or anything of that kind. I could hardly hope to succeed where you have failed, after all! But then it's in everyone's interests to catch this blighter, don't you think?'

'It's certainly in the interests of every law-abiding citizen,' said Mackenzie, carefully keeping his voice level. 'Fire away, Mr Raffles, I'm listening!'

'Well, at first I thought that Madame Carati might be involved — '

'Oh!'

'But I soon rejected that. No, it has all the marks of a one-man job, don't you agree?'

'One man, maybe. Or two,' said Mackenzie, turning his head slowly to look at me. I felt my face begin to burn, and lit a cigarette, cupping it in my hands to hide my emotions.

'One,' said Raffles confidently. 'Anyway, our man must be someone who is interested in Spiritualism, for otherwise he could never know just who would be away from home at any given time. Agreed?'

Mackenzie nodded. 'Agreed.'

'Next, he must be someone who was not at the meetings or seances which took place on the nights of the various robberies, for otherwise he could never commit the crimes. Agreed?'

'Agreed a second time.'

'Well?'

'Well, Mr Raffles?'

'Oh, Mr Mac! You have obviously been making enquiries, you must have a list of names, something of that sort?'

'And if I have?'

'Look here, Inspector,' said Raffles earnestly, 'Bunny and I are positively bending over backwards to help you catch this fellow. Won't you trust us just a little?'

'Well, maybe that's only fair.' Mackenzie reached into his jacket pocket and took out his notebook. 'I had a fairly lengthy list to begin with,' he said, 'but I was able to eliminate many of the names on it. Your name was on there, Mr Raffles,' he added casually.

'Mine?' Raffles looked astounded; he was, as I have often remarked, a superb actor.

'Oh, purely as a matter of form, you understand. I was able to cross you off at once — at once, sir — when I learned that you were at a seance at the time when one of the robberies took place.'

'Ah.' Raffles looked relieved. 'That's all right, then. You had me worried for a moment, Mr Mac! And the names you could not eliminate?'

'It boils down to three, Mr Raffles. Mr Raphael Mantini — '

'Who, despite his name, is an Englishman. Young chap, man about town,' Raffles said for my benefit.

'I know him well,' I replied.

'Aye,' said Mackenzie. 'He spends freely, but nobody seems to know just where he gets his money.'

'Oh, we are all in the same boat there!' said Raffles.

'Maybe so. Mr Mantini shows an interest in Spiritualism, attends the occasional seance, but he was not present at any that we know of when the robberies took place. Next, Mr James Dawson; same as Mr Mantini, give or take. And last, Dr Aloysius Boyle.'

'Dr Boyle!' It was out before I could think about it. 'Why, he's the greatest sceptic of the age, where Spiritualism is concerned! Won't have it at any price!'

'That's so,' nodded Mackenzie. 'But yet he knows everyone who is concerned in the business, he attends occasional seances, just like the other two, and, just like the other two, Dr Boyle was not at a seance when the robberies took place. Well, Mr Raffles, Mr Manders? Who do you back?'

'Mantini!' I said confidently; I had quite forgotten my scruples, since neither Raffles nor I had anything to fear from Mackenzie, and I entered into the spirit of the thing. 'Despite the fact that he's English of the English, he has an Italian ancestry, and that's the nation that produced Machiavelli. He probably has links with the Camorra, or something,' I added.

'H'mm,' said Mackenzie, clearly unimpressed — his own dour Scots ancestry showing itself, no doubt. 'Mr Raffles?'

'Oh, I'm not betting, Mr Mac. The three runners start even, as far as I'm concerned. Well, your course of action is pretty clear, I should think?'

'Aye.' Mackenzie hesitated. 'And in my place, what would you do, Mr Raffles?'

'Two things,' said Raffles. 'First, follow those three, especially when there's a seance!'

Mackenzie nodded. 'I shall,' he said. 'Second?'

'Second, I should try to work out just where the next robbery will take place.'

Mackenzie raised an eyebrow. 'Easier said than done, don't you think?'

'Not necessarily.' Raffles produced a piece of paper — but he used a different pencil this time. He scribbled away happily, then handed the sheet to Mackenzie. 'I have what you might call advance information this time, Mr Mac. Those are the people whom I know will

attend the next seance at Miss Ellison's
— you know her, of course? — on
Tuesday next. Now, who amongst those is
worthy of the attentions of a crook?'

Mackenzie studied the list, then handed
it to me. 'What's your opinion, Mr Manders?'

'No good asking me, Inspector!' I said
as innocently as I could manage. 'I don't
know these things, you know!'

'Of course not, Mr Manders.
Whatever was I thinking?' Mackenzie
studied the list closely. 'Well, now, Colonel Washburton, he has a fine collection of
Egyptian antiquities. Miss Young, porcelain. And — '

'And?' asked Raffles innocently.

'Oh, I fancied there was another name
I'd heard — but that's neither here nor
there. Yes, Mr Raffles, that's a good idea
of yours.' Mackenzie stood up. 'I'll say
good day, then, and thank you for your
help. By the way, Mr Raffles,' he added
as he took his hat and coat from the peg,
'will you be at the seance on Tuesday
yourself?'

'Well, I had intended to be there. But if
you'd rather I came along with you, I

could. I'd rather like to see the fun,' said Raffles.

'Not at all, not at all! These things are best left to us, Mr Raffles! You go along to see your young lady. And the spirits,' and Mackenzie grinned evilly and let himself out.

'Phew!' I reached for the brandy. 'Raffles, I hope never to have such an interview as that again!'

'Oh, I don't know, Bunny. It wasn't so bad, was it? By the way, Mackenzie seemed to think there was a third name on my list that might interest a crook. I wonder who that might be? Someone who has some secret store of valuables, and has asked Mackenzie to keep an eye open, I suppose? I'll have to make my own discreet enquiries there, for future reference, as it were. So that was an added bonus, Bunny! But even without that snippet of information, Mackenzie has done us a good turn.'

I frowned. 'Has he?'

'Of course he has. Mackenzie is no fool; I trust his judgement almost as much as I trust my own. If Mackenzie has identified Mantini, Dawson and Boyle as possibles, you may be sure that one of them is our crook. I confess I'd never have thought of Boyle myself, either, for he is such a sceptic about Spiritualism.'

'But — '

'Meantime, I shall have to usher you out, for I have some letters to write. Can you attend the seance on Tuesday?' he added.

'Me?'

'It might be as well. It is due to start at eight, so if you call here for me at seven-thirty?'

'If you wish, Raffles. Delighted, of course. Incidentally, do you think that Mackenzie was fooled? Do you think he sees us as decent citizens outraged by these dastardly crimes?'

Raffles threw back his head and laughed out loud. 'Hardly, Bunny! No, I imagine that Mackenzie has spotted the truth, or something very close to it. He, I imagine, sees us as hardened villains who — just this once! — happen to be innocent, and who want to see the real crook caught in order to eliminate the competition. And that's not so far from the reality, is it?'

'Raffles!'

'Well, I am a tradesman, Bunny, and like any other I must outdo my rivals in business whenever I can. Still, I should be careful what I did and who I saw, if I were you.'

'Raffles?'

'Oh, Mackenzie will have us both followed, you may be sure of that! He is not quite that trusting!'

'Really, Raffles!'

'Now, run along, and I'll expect you at seven-thirty on Tuesday.'

★ ★ ★

Prompt at seven-thirty on the Tuesday, I knocked on Raffles' door, and he let me in. 'Hullo, Bunny!' He glanced down the corridor. 'Been followed?'

'Raffles! Don't even joke about it.' I shivered. 'Now you mention it, I did have a curious feeling that someone was watching me.'

'Oh? I haven't, or not thus far. I suspect

that Mr Mac is half convinced of my innocence. But only half — I expect we'll be followed from here, just to make sure that we actually attend as advertised.'

We set off on foot, for Miss Ellison's house was at no great distance, in Mayfair. I had that curious sensation of being followed, and turned round abruptly before we had gone many yards.

'Stop that, you ass!' hissed Raffles.

'But — '

'Yes, of course we're being followed!' he said in the same low voice. 'We expected that, did we not? But, since we are innocent, we have nothing to fear, and can stride out confidently like any other honest citizens.' And he suited his actions to the word, making me half run to catch up; I spotted our 'shadow' also trying to keep pace, and at the same time trying to look as if he were nothing to do with us. This cheered me considerably, and I determined to enjoy the evening.

We arrived at Miss Ellison's, and Raffles introduced me to our hostess. Somehow or other I had formed the impression that the elder Miss Ellison was a short, stout, motherly body, similar in looks to Her Majesty Queen Victoria, but in reality she was as tall as Raffles, lean, with a cynical eye and an incisive turn of phrase. In fact she looked a jolly sight too knowing to be fooled by Spiritualism; which just goes to prove that you can't judge by appearances. 'Your first seance, Mr Manders?' she said to me. 'Well, sir, I trust you will not be disappointed. You have met my daughter? And this — this is Madame Carati.'

There was almost reverence in Miss Ellison's voice, and I studied the famous medium with some interest. And some disappointment, I might add, for she was positively dowdy; she reminded me of nothing so much as one of the aged flower sellers you see outside the theatre. Like Mr Raphael Mantini, she had an English accent, but unlike him she had the unmistakable suggestion of the East End in her tones. I mention Mr Mantini because he was there, too, somewhat to my surprise.

Miss Ellison was saying, 'So unusual! I

invite Mr Mantini and Mr Dawson to all these little affairs, and as a rule they refuse politely. Yet here they both are!' and she introduced me to Mr James Dawson, a pleasant enough young chap, whom I had never met until that evening. 'And,' added Miss Ellison, with the intonation of the true lion-hunter, 'we have a very rare treat indeed this evening! Dr Boyle seldom consents to attend any sort of Spiritualist gathering, yet here he is at my little party!' and she waved a hand to indicate the famous scientist and sceptic.

I had never met Dr Boyle, but I would easily have recognized the great mane of hair and bushy beard, familiar from the illustrations in the popular press, even without Miss Ellison's introduction.

His voice was a great bass rumble. 'I seldom attend because I know I am unwelcome,' he said to the room at large. 'The truth is unpalatable to the charlatans who infest this murky world — no offence, madam,' he added as Madame Carati looked set to contradict this. 'I am sure you yourself are quite genuine; but some are not.'

Madame Carati simpered. 'I'm sure I'm very flattered that you think so highly of my poor abilities, sir.'

Boyle frowned. 'H'mm. The truth is, I should not have been here had I not received a most curious letter.'

Mantini started visibly. 'You did? I had a letter, too. Said I should move heaven and earth to attend, as I should find out something that would interest me.'

'That is the same as mine!' said Dr Boyle. 'Exactly that wording!'

'Me, too!' added Mr James Dawson, producing an envelope from his pocket and waving it in the air.

Miss Ellison was staring from one to the other of them. 'Three mysterious letters, summoning you to my little gathering? You, who so seldom attend such things? You know, if I did not know better, I should wonder whether those letters were not written by — by a Spirit Hand!'

'I am quite convinced,' said Raffles calmly. And when I turned a sceptical gaze upon him, he kicked my ankle savagely. 'And you, Bunny?'

'Oh, rather! You can practically smell the spirits coming from those letters from here!'

Miss Ellison, still looking very ethereal, introduced me to the rest of her guests. There were half a dozen there, some of whom I knew, though most were strangers to me. I recognized the names of Colonel Washburton and Miss Young, the potential victims whom Mackenzie had identified. But if the colonel or Miss Young were to be robbed, how on earth could Mantini, or Dawson, or Boyle, assuming that one of these were the burglar, possibly rob them? And come to that, why were Messrs Mantini, Dawson and Boyle here at all? They were not on the original list of potential guests at the seance, the list which Raffles had produced for Inspector Mackenzie. And judging by the way the three of them had spoken, none of them would have attended the seance had they not each received a mysterious letter!

Well, even I was not quite that stupid; it

was fairly clear that Raffles himself must have written those letters! But why, when he meant to identify one of the three as the burglar? Unless he hoped that one of the three would somehow give himself away at the seance? But how?

I gave it up, partly because it was beyond me, and partly because Miss Dora Ellison now appeared to tell us that all was ready for the seance. I followed Raffles into a sitting room lit only by a single candle, and sat down as instructed, between Raffles and Miss Dora.

Do not ask me to give any detailed account of the proceedings; I know that the candle was blown out once we were all seated, and I know that Madame Carati made some odd noises before passing on on one or two messages supposedly from what she insisted on calling 'the dear departed.' Pretty trivial and rubbishy stuff they were too, those messages, but there were little gasps of surprise or satisfaction as Aunt Gladys said that so-and-so was not to worry, as all would be well on the other side, and that kind of thing.

The one surprise came towards the end of the session. Madame Carati had been silent for a couple of minutes, but then she suddenly let out a loud gasp, and called out, in the purest Cockney, 'Oh Gaw' blimey! What are you up to, then? Help, police!' and then there was another gasp, and she added, in her normal voice, 'Someone at this table has been robbed, this very evening!' then there was a crash, and everyone started talking at once.

Miss Dora and Miss Ellison scrambled round, lighting candles, and then the gas lamps, and we all looked at Madame Carati, who was rubbing her head — I rather think she had swooned and banged her forehead on the table, that being the crash I'd heard, but she was too overcome to bother about that. 'Never,' she told us, 'never, in all my professional career, have I had a message from the other side with such clarity! One of you here has certainly been robbed this evening! And perhaps more than one of you! I'll stake my professional reputation upon it!'

The Spiritualists were all convinced, and even the sceptical Dr Boyle could not be too sceptical; Madame Carati spoke with such absolute certainty. Even I was impressed, and wondered just what was going on. Only Raffles, imperturbable as ever, asked, 'Wonder who it might be?'

I saw Colonel Washburton give a little start, and Miss Young burst into tears.

'Perhaps,' Raffles added, 'it might be as well to conclude the seance now, and let each one of us check our possessions?' There was a move to second this, led, as you might have guessed, by the colonel and Miss Young.

Raffles had to say good evening to Miss Dora, of course, so he and I were about the last to go. As we reached the pavement, Mackenzie materialized from out of the shadows, like the best of apparitions.

'Why, Mr Mac!' said Raffles. 'Any luck?'

'None whatever, Mr Raffles,' Mackenzie said through his clenched teeth. 'The colonel's antiquities are safe, as is Miss Young's porcelain. I've had their premises watched carefully all evening, and those of another person I won't name, and there's been nothing untoward.'

'Well, that's a blessing!'

'Aye, maybe. But d'you know what I find curious, Mr Raffles?'

'What's that, Inspector?'

'All of the five men — I beg your pardon, the three men, three, of course — whom I thought might have had something to do with these robberies, were here this evening! Now, how do you explain that, Mr Raffles?'

'I'm sure I can't,' said Raffles vaguely. 'They're all interested in Spiritualism, you know. And then, my little theory was just that, a theory. As I said, I couldn't hope to succeed where Scotland Yard had failed, could I?'

Mackenzie snorted. 'A wild-goose chase, Mr Raffles!'

'But — '

'And I have to say, sir — and I say it with some regret, for I can find it in me to admire you — that I hold you personally responsible for the waste of my time, and that of my officers!'

'Come, now, Mr Mac! I acted in good faith, after all. Why, in pursuit of the truth, Bunny and I have been sitting through two hours of Spiritualist nonsense — '

'Spiritualist nonsense!'

I shrank back at the roar from behind us, and even Raffles' imperturbability was shaken. We turned to see Miss Ellison and Miss Dora standing in the lighted doorway.

'Spiritualist nonsense?' said Miss Ellison again in stentorian tones. She seemed set to say more, but words evidently failed her. She turned on her heel with a good deal of contempt, putting an arm round her niece. 'Come away, Dora.' As she started to close the door, Miss Ellison added, 'Mr Raffles, I trust that it it is quite unnecessary for me to say — '

Raffles bowed. 'Consider it said, madam.' He gazed ruefully at me, then at Inspector Mackenzie, as the door slammed loudly. 'Well, I seem to have come very badly out of this!' But I fancied that I could detect relief in his voice.

'Well,' said Mackenzie awkwardly, 'I see you've lost your young lady over the matter, so we'll maybe say no more about it. Good evening to you, gentlemen.'

We set off for the Albany. 'I'm sorry about Miss Dora,' I began.

'Oh, these things happen,' said Raffles, untroubled. 'Truth to tell, Bunny, that Spiritualist rubbish was beginning to get a trifle wearing, you know. A pity in some ways, for she was — is — a most attractive girl!'

'Madame Carati seems to have slipped up, too,' I added. 'And we still don't know who the burglar is.'

'You know, that Carati business was odd,' said Raffles. 'Makes you think there might be something in it, after all. I wonder how she knew?'

'Knew what? Nobody was robbed, were they?'

'Weren't they?'

I stared at him. 'Were they? But Mantini and the others were there! Can't have been any one of them, can it, even if someone was robbed this evening?'

'Oh, it was Boyle,' said Raffles, in an offhand fashion.

'Boyle? But — '

'I've told you often enough, Bunny,

337

that a man in this profession of ours must have a public life, the more prominent the better. Boyle was the obvious choice, when you think about it. With his outspoken attitude to Spiritualists, and charlatans, and what have you, he's always appearing in the papers, and that provides a perfect cover for his other work.'

'But Boyle was sitting opposite us, Raffles! It cannot possibly have been him this evening, if anyone was robbed, which I doubt!'

'Oh, not this evening, Bunny. Not this evening. That was me. And that's how I know it was Boyle who committed the other robberies. I recovered the loot, which he hadn't yet sold.' And he took a handful of jewels from a pocket. 'Old Mrs Waterman's necklace, Bunny. And here we have Colonel Browne's Roman coins. I suspect that the 'Spiritualist robberies' will cease immediately; Boyle won't want to run the risk of doing any more, now he knows that someone else knows that he's the crook. That means Mackenzie will leave us alone, my Bunny.'

I was frankly puzzled. 'But you can't — well, you must have, because you did! But you can't have robbed him during the seance, because you were there, too!'

'Of course I was there. And of course I robbed him before the seance. Whilst he was dressing for dinner, as a matter of fact.'

'You mean that he was in the house whilst you — '

Raffles nodded. 'I had to be deuced careful, of course. He being a crook himself, he would be extra vigilant. And of course I knew that Mackenzie's men were watching him! And for all I knew they were very likely watching — or trying to watch — me, too! I tell you, Bunny, I have had some anxious moments this evening! Still, no harm done. That reminds me, I'd better leave you here, and dispose of my swag.'

'No hurry, surely, Raffles? Boyle is hardly likely to call the police in, after all! He cannot tell them that his ill-gotten gains have been stolen by another crook!'

'Oh, Boyle won't call the police. But Mantini and Dawson will. You see,

339

Bunny, I didn't know for certain at the outset that it was Boyle. It could equally well have been one of the other two. So I paid them all three a visit this evening, and, once inside, it seemed a pity to leave empty handed!'

THE END

We do hope that you have enjoyed reading this large print book.

Did you know that all of our titles are available for purchase?

We publish a wide range of high quality large print books including:
Romances, Mysteries, Classics
General Fiction
Non Fiction and Westerns

Special interest titles available in large print are:
The Little Oxford Dictionary
Music Book, Song Book
Hymn Book, Service Book

Also available from us courtesy of Oxford University Press:
Young Readers' Dictionary
(large print edition)
Young Readers' Thesaurus
(large print edition)

For further information or a free brochure, please contact us at:
Ulverscroft Large Print Books Ltd.,
The Green, Bradgate Road, Anstey,
Leicester, LE7 7FU, England.
Tel: (00 44) **0116 236 4325**
Fax: (00 44) **0116 234 0205**

DEAD FOR DANGER

Lorette Foley

When a young Dublin woman is mugged and afterwards stabbed, the police look in vain for the attacker. But 49 Organ Place, the seedy apartment house where she lived, holds the secret which links her fate with that of a desperate and hunted man . . . Detective Inspector Moss Coen is baffled by the discovery of another body. But when all the tenants suffer a final, devastating and deadly attack, the Inspector must go all out to find a merciless killer.

DEATH IN SILHOUETTE

John Russell Fearn

Maria Black, headmistress-detective, is invited to the engagement celebrations of an ex-pupil — and becomes involved in the apparent suicide of the prospective bridegroom, Keith Robinson. The circumstances — death by hanging in a locked cellar — satisfy the coroner that Robinson took his own life. However, 'Black Maria' thinks otherwise, and sets out, with her companion 'Pulp' Martin, to prove how Keith really died. She uncovers a plan of cold-blooded murder. But who is the killer — and why was Robinson killed?

RUN WITH THE FOX

Craig Cooper

In a world of rigid discipline and backbreaking toil, life is tough for Lew Ames at the prison farm. Fellow convict Mel Savage's objective is the recovery of a quarter million dollars. Ames' release date is near — and if he helps Savage, there's a half share of the cash in it for him . . . But when a man runs with the fox he can never expect his life to be easy. For sudden death will follow should his mission fail . . .